# A LIST OF THE ELSIE BOOKS AND OTHER POPULAR BOOKS

BY

## MARTHA FINLEY

ELSIE DINSMORE.
ELSIE'S HOLIDAYS AT ROSELANDS.
ELSIE'S GIRLHOOD.
ELSIE'S WOMANHOOD.
ELSIE'S MOTHERHOOD.
ELSIE'S CHILDREN.
ELSIE'S WIDOWHOOD.
GRANDMOTHER ELSIE.
ELSIE'S NEW RELATIONS.
ELSIE AT NANTUCKET.
THE TWO ELSIES.
ELSIE'S KITH AND KIN.
ELSIE'S FRIENDS AT WOODBURN.
CHRISTMAS WITH GRANDMA ELSIE.
ELSIE AND THE RAYMONDS.
ELSIE YACHTING WITH THE RAYMONDS.
ELSIE'S VACATION.
ELSIE AT VIAMEDE.
ELSIE AT ION.
ELSIE AT THE WORLD'S FAIR.
ELSIE'S JOURNEY ON INLAND WATERS.
ELSIE AT HOME.
ELSIE ON THE HUDSON.
ELSIE IN THE SOUTH.
ELSIE'S YOUNG FOLKS.
ELSIE'S WINTER TRIP.
ELSIE AND HER LOVED ONES.
ELSIE AND HER NAMESAKES.

MILDRED KEITH.
MILDRED AT ROSELANDS.
MILDRED'S MARRIED LIFE.
MILDRED AND ELSIE.
MILDRED AT HOME.
MILDRED'S BOYS AND GIRLS.
MILDRED'S NEW DAUGHTER.

CASELLA.
SIGNING THE CONTRACT AND WHAT IT COST.
THE TRAGEDY OF WILD RIVER VALLEY.
OUR FRED.
AN OLD-FASHIONED BOY.
WANTED, A PEDIGREE.
THE THORN IN THE NEST.

# ELSIE AT ION

BY

MARTHA FINLEY

NEW YORK
DODD, MEAD & COMPANY
PUBLISHERS

# ELSIE AT ION.

## CHAPTER I.

VIOLET and Lulu were still alone upon the veranda where the captain had left them while he drove into the village on that first evening after their home-coming from beautiful Viamede. They had now taken possession of two easy-chairs standing close together, and were enjoying the quiet and an extended view of the well-kept grounds and the green fields and wooded hills that lay beyond.

For some moments neither had spoken; then Violet broke the silence. "Lulu, I have been thinking of that poor Mrs. McAlpine and her daughter whom you met when your father took you and Max out to the far West. Tell me something about them if you feel inclined."

"Yes, Mamma Vi; they were refined, lovable people and I like to think and talk of them; except that it makes me sad to think what a hard, trying life they led and are yet leading, I suppose."

"Yes, my heart bleeds for them; the poor mother especially," sighed Violet. "Foully robbed of her husband's love, what charm has life in this world left for her?"

"If I were in her place I'd just make up my mind not to care for him or his love, and be happy in loving my children and being loved by them!" exclaimed Lulu in indignant tones. "I'd never break my heart for such a wretch!"

"He is certainly not worth it," was Violet's response. "Ah, there is your father!" as a carriage turned in at the great gates opening upon the high-road.

It came swiftly up the drive, halted at the front entrance, and the captain, quickly alighting, handed out a girlish figure clad in a plain, dark dress and hat.

"Miss McAlpine, my dear; Lulu, it is your old friend Marian."

"Welcome, my poor dear girl," said Violet, taking Marian's hand in a kindly pressure and giving her a kiss.

"O Marian, Marian, what a delightful surprise!" was Lulu's greeting as she threw her arms about her friend and kissed her again and again.

"Just as I meant it should be," the captain remarked with a pleased smile.

But Marian seemed speechless with emotion,

clinging to Lulu and sobbing as if her heart would break.

"O you poor dear!" Lulu said, gently patting and stroking her, "don't cry so bitterly; we will do all we can to make you happy. You must be very tired with your long journey, but you can rest now in this sweet home of ours."

"Yes, take her up to the spare room nearest your own, Lulu," said the captain, "and see that she has everything she needs."

"And we will have her tea sent up to her," added Violet.

"She took that in the village, my dear," said the captain, "and as she is very weary had better get to bed as soon as she can. I see that her trunk has already been carried up."

"O sir, how kind, how kind you are to me!" Marian exclaimed sobbingly, putting her hand into his and lifting grateful eyes to his face.

"Ah, my poor child, it would be a great delight to me could I but relieve all your sorrows," he returned in moved tones. "That is beyond my power; but cast all your burdens on the Lord and he will sustain you, fulfilling to you his gracious promise, 'As thy days, so shall thy strength be.' You need rest; do not lie awake grieving, but try to obey the scriptural injunction, 'casting all your care upon him, for he careth for you.'"

"O sir, I believe it!" Marian responded in deeply grateful tones; "for otherwise he would never have raised up such a friend as you are proving yourself to be. How shall I ever thank one who shows himself far kinder than my own father?"

"Yes, my dear girl, my good husband feels for you very much as he does for his own children when they are in trouble," Violet said feelingly, as Marian turned to say good-night to her. "Lulu, dear," she added, "try to make sure that your guest has everything that can add to her comfort."

"I will, Mamma Vi," Lulu answered in pleasant tones.

"And stay with Marian only long enough to see to that," added the captain; "for her journey has fatigued her greatly and she needs rest more than anything else."

"Yes, sir; we can wait till to-morrow for our talk," Lulu replied, looking smilingly up into his face; "and I'll come directly to you so that you will know I have obeyed the order."

"That is right; you will find me here," he returned.

"Oh, what a lovely home you have, Lulu!" exclaimed Marian, glancing about her as they went up the stairway.

"Yes, indeed, I think we have; and I love it

dearly; but not a thousandth part as much as I do the dear father who made it for us and makes us so happy in it. This is the room he bade me bring you to, Marian," opening a door and leading the way into a large, airy, and beautifully furnished bedroom.

"Oh, how lovely, how lovely!" exclaimed Marian. "Ah, it is much too grand for me —a poor girl who has not a dollar in the world."

"Not a bit," said Lulu in reply; "those who have nothing need help all the more; besides, papa does not value people for their wealth and has never taught his children to. Ah, there is your trunk! I see the men have unstrapped it. Now if you are too tired to get out the things you want for to-night, and will give me the key, I will do so for you while you sit here in this easy-chair and direct me."

"Oh, thank you! but I feel able to wait on myself."

"Well, you shall do exactly as you please," returned Lulu with a smile. "I see the servants have filled your pitchers, and if you should want anything that is not here, you have only to touch this knob which rings an electric bell in the kitchen—giving it one push for cold, or two for hot water, or three for the chambermaid to come to you."

"How very nice and convenient!" exclaimed Marian.

Lulu then explained about the light, saying she was welcome to put it out or leave it burning just as she preferred, and bidding her a kind good-night left the room. Hurrying down to the veranda, she found her father and Violet still there sitting side by side, conversing together in rather subdued tones.

"Here I am, papa," Lulu said, approaching them.

"That is right," he responded and drew her to a seat upon his knee. "You saw that your guest had every want supplied?" he asked, caressing her hair and cheek with his hand as he spoke.

"Yes, sir. O papa, tell me all about it, please."

"All about what?" he asked with a smile, holding her close and pressing a kiss upon her lips.

"About Marian, sir. Did you know she was coming? and was it just to get her you drove into the village?"

"One question at a time, my child," he returned with an amused look. "Yes, I knew she was coming. I had found a letter from her on my library table telling me so, and reminding me of the invitation you heard me give her just before leaving Minersville, to apply to me for help should the time ever come when she would need a friend able and willing to aid her."

"Oh, yes, papa, I remember it, and I don't think anybody could find a better friend than my dear father when in need of one."

"Well, I found the letter, read it to your Mamma Vi, then drove into the village for Marian, leaving for you the pleasure of being taken by surprise on seeing her return with me."

"And a very pleasant surprise it was, papa. Is she going to stay? and oh, what has become of her poor mother and the boys? I suppose she told you all about them as you drove back from the village?"

"More than two questions at once this time," laughed her father. "I will try to answer them in turn. She is likely to stay with us for the present at least. Her mother and all the younger children, except Sandy, are dead; the little ones dying of diphtheria, the mother of grief and the fatigue from nursing them through their illness. Sandy is working his way with a farmer for the present; the father attempted to force Marian into a match with a Mormon thirty or forty years older than herself, and she, by running away, barely escaped a fate that she esteemed far worse than death."

"Oh, poor thing!" cried Lulu. "How glad I am that I have a father who would never force me to leave him for anybody else," clinging still closer to him as she spoke.

"Never, no, never, my own precious child!" he returned with emotion. "But you are still far too young even to be thinking of such a thing."

"Yes, I know that, papa, and I'm glad of it. I like to be a little girl that nobody wants to get away from her father."

"Then we are both satisfied."

"Papa, is Marian going to live here with us?" she asked.

"Nothing is decided yet," he replied, "but it will depend upon circumstances. Would you wish it, daughter?"

She hesitated a little, then said: "If you and Mamma Vi want her here, papa, I would not like to stand in the way of her having such a sweet home, but—it's so delightful to have our dear home to ourselves; just you and Mamma Vi and us children."

"So your mamma and I think," he returned with a gratified look; "and very possibly Marian herself would prefer some other plan, for I perceive she is of a very independent disposition. I have learned that it is her desire and purpose to earn her own living, and I think

the kindest thing I can do will be to help her
fit herself for whatever work she may think
best suited to her talents and inclination."

"O papa, take her for one of your pupils,
won't you?" cried Lulu in her most eager,
coaxing tones.

"If she wishes it, and can be located in the
near neighborhood," he said.

"Oh, I have a thought!" exclaimed Lulu.
"Why can't she live with Mrs. Allen and Susie
at the cottage?"

"Ah, that strikes me as a very good suggestion," the captain replied. "What do you
think of it, Violet, my dear?"

"I highly approve," returned Violet, "unless
it may crowd them too much."

"Ah, in that case I can easily add another
room, or two of them if deemed desirable," he
said. "They might stand a little crowding for
a time, till they satisfy themselves as to their
congeniality of disposition—for even good people sometimes find that they are more comfortable apart than thrown constantly together;
and that having been satisfactorily proved, I
would make the addition. But we need decide
nothing in regard to these matters to-night.
There is the bell for prayers, after which Lulu
must go to her nest, and you and I, my dear,
will, I think, be ready for ours."

When the short service was over, Lulu bade Violet good-night; then turning to her father, asked, "Must I say it to you too now, papa?"

"No, daughter," he replied. "I will step in your room for a moment when you are about ready for bed. I suppose it would hardly do to omit it on the first night after our return from our wanderings," he added, smoothing her hair caressingly as she stood by his side.

"No, indeed, sir," she returned with an earnestness that made him smile; "and please do not think it will do at any time; unless you are sick or have some company you cannot leave to give me even a minute. Ah, how thankful I ought to be, and am, that my father is so different from poor Marian's!"

"Yes, indeed," said Violet. "Marian, poor girl, is greatly to be pitied; so let us all be as kind to her as possible."

"Yes, Mamma Vi; and I think it will be my place to stay with her to-morrow, though I shall be very sorry to miss spending the after-noon and evening with the rest of you at Ion."

"You dear girl, you shall do no such thing," returned Violet with an affectionate smile into Lulu's eyes. "I will speak to mamma through the telephone to-morrow morning, and I am sure she will give Marian a cordial invitation to make one of the family party."

"I do not doubt it, my dear," said Captain Raymond, "but in her fatigue and grief Marian would, I think, prefer to spend the day here in rest and sleep; nor will there be any occasion for Lulu to deny herself the pleasure of going with the rest of us to Ion, or us the pleasure of having her along," again laying a caressing hand upon her head and smiling down affectionately into the bright dark eyes lifted lovingly to his. "Now go, daughter, to your room. I want you to have a good night's rest that you may enjoy the pleasures of to-morrow to the full."

# CHAPTER II.

"Ah, how I wish poor dear Marian was blessed with such a father as mine," Lulu said to herself as she moved noiselessly about her room getting ready for bed. "But I doubt if there is another quite so dear and good—though Mamma Vi says hers was, and Grandma Elsie seems to think hers could not possibly be excelled! The idea! I'm as glad as can be that I wasn't born his child, though the older he grows the better and kinder he seems to be. And that's the way it ought to be with all of us; papa says so, and I know it's according to Bible teachings. 'Grow in grace, and in the knowledge of our Lord and Saviour Jesus Christ,' it says. Ah me! there's nobody needs to do that more than you yourself, you bad-tempered, wilful Lulu Raymond. I am glad you have a father who understands the business of training you up in the way you should go, as well as mine does," and presently, when he came in, she turned to him with a remark to that effect.

"If I have succeeded in training my children

at all in the right way, it is only by the wisdom given me of God in answer to earnest prayer for it," he replied with grave earnestness. "Now good-night, my dear little daughter," again laying a hand tenderly upon her head. "'The Lord bless thee and keep thee; the Lord make his face to shine upon thee, and be gracious unto thee; the Lord lift up his countenance upon thee, and give thee peace.'"

"Dear papa, thank you," she said, lifting dewy eyes to his; "it is such a beautiful, beautiful blessing!"

"It is indeed! the blessing which the Lord directed Moses to give to Aaron and his sons to use in blessing the children of Israel; adding 'and they shall put my name upon the children of Israel, and I will bless them.' Now again good-night, daughter. Get to bed and to sleep as quickly as you can."

Lulu obeyed, and her head had scarcely more than touched the pillow before her senses were lost in sound sleep, from which she did not awake till just as the sun appeared above the tree-tops.

"Oh, what a lovely morning! everything looking so beautiful within and without!" she exclaimed to herself, glancing around the handsomely furnished room, then out at the beautiful grounds. "Ah, I want a morning stroll with my dear father!" and with the words she sprang from the bed and began a hasty but neat toilet; but first she laid her Bible open on the dressing-table that she might commit a verse or more to memory as she worked.

Then a few moments were spent on her knees giving thanks for God's protecting care over her and hers during the silent watches of the night, the many, many blessings of her lot in life, and the hope of eternal life through the righteousness and atoning blood of Christ, confessing her sins, asking forgiveness for Jesus' sake, and help to love him more and serve him better.

Grace still slept soundly, as Lulu discovered on peeping in at the open door communicating with her own room. Polly woke and called for a cracker, according to her custom. Lulu gave her one, told her to be silent and not disturb tired sleepers, then passed quietly out to the hall and to Marian's door, where she stood listening till satisfied that no movement was going on within that room; then seeing her father passing out of his dressing-room into the hall, she ran to him, was welcomed with a smile and a kiss, slipped her hand into his, and they went down the stairs together.

"Have you had anything to eat?" he asked, adding, "It will be more than an hour yet before we are called to breakfast, and that will make too long a fast from the time you must have left your bed."

"No, sir, I haven't," she replied. "Shall I call for a glass of milk for you and one for myself?"

"Suppose instead we take a basket and go out to the strawberry bed. How would you like that?" he asked.

"Oh, ever so much, papa!" she exclaimed delightedly. "And might we not gather some for breakfast too? Mamma Vi and the rest will enjoy them as well as you and I."

"I entirely approve of the suggestion," he returned, and they set off together for the strawberry patch.

It was a large one supplied with an abundance of the finest varieties, the vines now loaded with delicious fruit just in prime condition for eating.

"Oh, how beautiful they are!" cried Lulu. "So many too, and so nicely arranged and trained that they don't get any sand at all on them; and so large that it won't take long to fill our basket, papa."

"No, not many minutes. Gather and eat all you wish and we will fill the basket afterward."

"Thank you, sir," she said, and hastened to avail herself of the permission. For some minutes she was too busy to talk, but at length, when the filling of the basket began, she broke the silence with a question: "Papa, did Marian tell you how she escaped from Miners-ville?"

"Yes," he replied; "and now you want me to tell you, I suppose?"

"Oh, yes, sir, if you will."

"I will tell you something about it, but let you get the particulars from Marian herself. My agent, Mr. Short, was a good friend to the poor girl, supplied her with funds and whatever else she needed; took her by night to a station some miles distant on the railroad, bought her a ticket, had her trunk checked, put her on board an eastern train and watched it out of sight."

"And she travelled all the rest of the way alone, papa?"

"Yes; as far as Union, where I met her with my carriage."

"I think she was very brave, papa; but any-thing was better than the fate she would have had if she had stayed where that wicked, cruel father of hers could have done what he pleased with her. Oh, how glad and thankful I am that God gave me such a good, kind father!"

"And I that you are mine," he returned with a loving look into her beaming eyes. "It speaks ill indeed for Mormonism that it can so harden the heart against those who should be regarded with the tenderest affection. There! we have filled our basket and now we will go back to the house."

The breakfast-bell rang just as they stepped into the veranda. Violet was there with the three younger children; morning greetings were exchanged, then all repaired to the breakfast-room.

"I think our weary young guest is still sleeping," Violet said. "I knocked softly at her door and listened for several minutes, but could hear no sound; so thought it best to let her sleep on and give her her breakfast when she wakes of herself."

"Quite right, my dear," returned the captain as he lifted baby Ned to his high chair, then seated himself.

He asked a blessing upon their food and the meal began. They were the usual cheerful little family party, chatting pleasantly among themselves while they ate.

As they rose from the table Violet said: "I think I will go to the telephone and have a little chat with mamma while the servants are eating."

"And may I go with you?" the captain asked with a smile.

"I shall be happy to have you, sir," she re-

2

turned with a laughing look up into his face. "The children are welcome to come, too, if they wish."

At Ion the family were about leaving the breakfast-table when the telephone bell rang. It was answered by Edward. "Hello! who is there? and what's wanted?"

"It is I. I wish to speak to mamma," was the reply in Violet's own sweet tones. "No objections to others hearing, though."

"Dear me, I hope she isn't going to say they can't come to-day!" exclaimed Rosie, while Edward stepped aside and their mother took the place he vacated.

"What is it, Vi?" she asked, and all listened intently for the reply.

"We have a guest, Marian McAlpine—that Minersville young girl you have all heard my husband, Max and Lu speak of."

"Ah! then bring her with you to-day, if she will come."

"Thank you, mamma; we will if she is able and willing to accompany us; she was greatly fatigued by her journey and seems to be still sleeping."

"McAlpine?" exclaimed Mr. Lilburn, standing near. "You and I have some distant relatives of that name, Cousin Elsie. Please ask for the father's first name."

"I have heard the captain say his wife called him Willie," Elsie answered.

"Ah, indeed!" exclaimed Mr. Lilburn, in a tone of some excitement. "I must see the lassie. Please say to Cousin Vi that I will be over there an hour hence. And will you not accompany me, cousin?"

"With pleasure," she replied, and turning to her father, "Shall we not make up a party, papa?" she asked.

"Yes," he said. "It is a lovely morning for a drive and we may as well do so, all going who have time and inclination."

"I wonder if our young guest is awake yet," Violet said to her husband as they turned away from the telephone. "Shall I send a servant up to see?"

"No, my dear, I think I wouldn't," the captain replied. "I told her last night to lie and sleep as late this morning as she would, ring for her breakfast when she was ready to eat it, and it should be carried up to her. Ah! there is her bell now. I will direct that it be taken up at once, and then we will have family worship."

On coming down nearly an hour later Marian found the family gathered upon the front veranda. The captain rose on her appearance and gallantly handed her to a seat, remarking that she was looking much better and brighter than on her arrival the previous evening.

"Yes, sir," she said, "and I feel far better. I was very weary with my long journey (what a very big country America is!), but I slept well and am almost rested now."

Just then a carriage was seen to turn in at the gates opening upon the high-road. Ned greeted its approach with a shout of delight.

"Gan'ma tumin'! gan'ma tumin'. Oh, I so blad, I so blad!"

"Yes, Neddie boy, we are always glad to see dear grandma," said his father. "Grandpa Dinsmore too, Cousin Ronald, Rosie and Walter. They are all there, I see."

The next minute the carriage had drawn up at the foot of the steps and the captain was assisting his guests to alight and bidding them heartily welcome.

Cousin Ronald, waiting only to greet Violet, turned to the young stranger guest, and grasping her hand said with emotion: "I need ask no questions, for that bonny, winsome face tells plainer than any words that you are my Cousin Janet's bairn."

Marian gazed at him for a moment in dumb astonishment; then a glad surprise lighted up her face.

"A kinsman of my dear mother?" she exclaimed.

"Yes, my bonny lass. Did you never hear her speak of her Cousin Ronald Lilburn?"

"Oh, I have, sir, I have! and you are he?"

"That I am, lassie; and old enough to be your grandsire; so dinna think it too great a liberty I take," kissing her on cheek and lip. "And my cousin Elsie here, and her children, may claim kindred with you also, lassie," putting the hand he held into that of Mrs. Travilla.

"Yes, we must be permitted to claim you as our own, dear girl," Grandma Elsie said in tender tones and with an affectionate caress. Then turning to her children, "Rosie and Walter," she said, "this is your cousin, too."

"Then mine also, mamma," exclaimed Violet. "Ah, Marian, I am glad to know there is such a tie between us!" taking the young girl's hand in hers and holding it for a moment in a kindly pressure.

"I also, for if related to my wife you are to me too," the captain said, laying a hand affectionately upon the young girl's shoulder.

Then the younger ones greeted her warmly in turn. Mr. Dinsmore shook hands with her in a kind, grandfatherly way, saying that she must no longer feel herself a stranger in a strange land, but that the God of her fathers had guided

her to an abiding-place among her own kith
and kin.

Marian seemed well-nigh overwhelmed with
joy and gratitude by the sudden glad change in
her condition, laughing and crying hysterically
in turn; but under the kind ministrations of
her newly found relatives soon recovered her
composure and was able to answer coherently
the many questions Cousin Ronald had to ask
concerning her parents and brothers.

His manner increased in gentleness and tenderness as he learned of her many and recent
bereavements and the cruel treatment received
at the hands of her unnatural father.

Mr. Lilburn's brow darkened as he listened.
"Ah, to think o' my ain bonny cousin throwing
hersel' awa upon sic a beast o' a mon!" he mut-
tered between his set teeth; then aloud to Marian, "Dinna fash yersel', lassie; the Lord has
blessed your Cousin Ronald wi' abundance o'
this worl's gude; sons too, and one married
daughter, but no single one now the two that
were once the pride and joy o' his heart having
been long since called to the Father's house on
high, and if it so pleases you he will be glad
to take you in the place of one of them."

"How very kind you are, sir!" she exclaimed
with starting tears. "I cannot consent to be a
burden to any one, but will gladly take help

to fit myself for some useful employment by which I can earn my daily bread."

"And that you shall have, my dear lass," he said emphatically.

"But we need not settle anything to-day," their Cousin Elsie remarked, then told Marian of the family gathering to be held at Ion that afternoon, adding a warm invitation to her to make one of the company.

Marian accepted with thanks; then, coloring and hesitating, said she feared she had nothing to wear which would be suitable for such an occasion.

"My dear girl, do not allow yourself to be troubled with any such fears," Elsie replied in gentle, reassuring accents. "It is only a family gathering, and the dress you are now wearing will be quite suitable."

"Surely, surely, lassie, it strikes me as far from unbecoming," Cousin Ronald said, regarding her and her apparel with critical eyes, "and if any in the company think ill o'e dress, let him or her forget it in gazing upon the bonny face above it."

"I think you need not feel ashamed of it or fear unfavorable criticism, my dear girl," added Violet.

"No, dress is but a secondary matter in the connection, so far as I know," said the captain, and Rosie and Lulu added their assurance to the same effect.

"Then I shall go with pleasure and try not to think of the dress at all," returned Marian with a look of relief.

Walter, ever ready for a story, had been eagerly watching his opportunity and now earnestly requested of Marian a detailed account of her escape from Minersville. She complied and gave the facts in a way that all her hearers found exceedingly interesting.

At the conclusion of her narrative the Ion callers departed, and after dinner the whole Woodburn family, including their guest, followed.

Marian's eyes were bright with happiness in the discovery that the captain and Lulu, both of whom she had learned to dearly love in the by-gone days of her acquaintance with them in the far West, were in some sort connected with her and disposed to treat her as a near and valued relative; also that through them she had come upon others actually of her mother's kith and kin and disposed to take her in among them and treat her as one of themselves. Ah, what a sudden and delightful change from the lonely and forlorn condition which had been hers but the day before!

She greatly enjoyed the short drive to Ion,

the warm welcome received there by herself as
well as the others, the pleasant, kindly greetings
of the different members of the various family
connections, all of whom, though many of them
were not actually even distantly related to her,
met her with the greatest cordiality and seemed
deeply interested in the story of her past and
her prospects for the future.

It was a great pleasure to make acquaintance
with the young girls from the Oaks, with Lora
Howard also and Evelyn Leland, with all of
whom she spent the greater part of the afternoon in pleasant chat, while wandering about
the beautiful grounds and boating on the lovely
lakelet.

While the young people strolled over the
grounds the older ones sat conversing together
in the veranda. Much of the talk was of
Marian and what could be done to help her to
a happy and useful life. It soon became ap-
parent that any one of them was ready to offer
her a home; Captain Raymond more than
willing to take her into the number of his
pupils, and Mr. Lilburn really anxious to bear
all the expense of her clothing and education.

"If she will accept me as her teacher the
education need cost but little," remarked Captain Raymond.

"And I," said Mrs. Elsie Travilla, "must

claim the privilege of supplying at least a part
of her clothing; for as my dear mother's relative she seems very near to me."

"And what is left for me to do?" asked Mr.
Lilburn with a comical look of chagrin and
dismay.

"Why, sir, you might supply pocket-money,"
suggested Zoe.

"Or settle a few thousands upon her so that
she need not feel absolutely penniless," added
Edward.

"Ah ha! ah ha! um hm! that's no so bad
an idea, cousin," returned the old gentleman
with a humorous look and smile; "and it is to
be hoped our bonny lassie may not be averse to
receiving it from 'a kinsman near, a clansman
true;' though the kin be not so near as one
might wish."

"Yet if you adopt her that need make but
little difference," Edward laughingly returned.

"Quite true, sir, and whether that is done or
no will rest wi' the sweet lassie hersel'," said
the old gentleman, relapsing into his Scottish
brogue. "She is one any man might be proud
to call his daughter."

"So we all think," said Elsie Leland, "and
Lester and I would be glad to give her a home
at Fairview. She would make a desirable companion for Evelyn, we think."

"She would do quite as well for Ella at the Roselands; wouldn't she, Cal?" said Dr. Arthur Conly with a humorous look at his elder brother.

"Not a doubt of it; for ourselves too, for that matter," laughed Calhoun.

"Or for us at the Oaks," remarked the younger Mr. Horace Dinsmore; and his sister Mrs. Lacey added, "Or for us at the Laurels."

"Evidently she is in no danger of finding herself homeless," remarked the father of the last two with a smile.

"No, indeed! not while her older Cousin Elsie has one or more to offer her," added the sweet voice of his eldest daughter. "I propose that some of us take her into the city to-morrow morning and buy for her whatever may be needed to supply her with a wardrobe equal to that of any one of our own girls."

"A very good thought, cousin," said Mr. Lilburn, "and with your leave I shall make one of that party. And might it not be well to take the lass herself with us and consult her own taste to supplement the good judgment of yourself and any of the other ladies who may care to accompany us?"

"And give her the pleasure of seeing the city too," said Zoe, "if she is sufficiently rested from her long and wearisome journey to enjoy it."

After a little more talk it was fully decided that the trip to the city and the shopping should be undertaken on the morrow, and Marian invited to accompany them or not, as might suit her inclination.

## CHAPTER III.

THE tea-hour drew near and the young folks came trooping in and joined their elders on the veranda. All had presently found seats and were chatting gayly with their elders or among themselves. Marian alone, occupying a chair close by Mr. Lilburn's side, was a silent though interested listener, until Captain Raymond, turning to her, asked in his pleasant tones how she liked Ion.

"O sir!" she exclaimed with enthusiasm, "it is lovely! lovely! but not any more beautiful than Woodburn."

"Ah! I am glad you like Woodburn also, because I want it to be one of your homes, and its school-room one of the places where you may get such an education as I know you want. Do you think you could content yourself with me for a tutor?"

"O sir! how kind you are to me!" she exclaimed with tears of joy in her eyes. "If you will accept me as a pupil I shall strive most earnestly to do credit to your teaching. But ah! I fear you will find me but a dull scholar, and teaching me much too heavy a tax upon your time and patience."

"Never fear," he returned pleasantly. "I incline to the opinion that I shall enjoy having one or more pupils. I think it will add interest to my work and take scarcely more of my time."

While this little conversation was being carried on, Cousin Ronald had caught a very wishful, entreating look from Walter, to which he had nodded a smiling assent, and now the loud warble of a bird, seemingly right in their midst, caught every eye and ear and all eyes turned toward the spot from which the sound seemed to come.

"Why, where is the birdie? I don't see it," exclaimed little Elsie as the sounds suddenly ceased.

"I 'spect it flewed away," cried little Ned, sending quick glances from side to side and overhead.

Walter's face was full of suppressed delight, but he dodged suddenly, putting up his hand to drive away a bee that seemed to be circling about his head, buzzing now at one ear, now at the other; then recalling the probable cause, he laughed aloud, others of the company joining in with him.

Marian, too, had heard the buzzing and was looking up and around for a bee, when a " Peep,

peep, peep!" close at hand made her look down and around upon the floor at her feet.

Her countenance expressed surprise and bewilderment that no chick was in sight.

"Peep, peep, peep!" came again, seemingly from her pocket or among the folds of her dress-skirt. She rose hastily to her feet, shook her skirts, then thrust her hand into her pocket.

"Why, where is it?" she asked, looking somewhat alarmed.

"Why, it seems to have come to me!" Grace Raymond exclaimed as the "Peep, peep, peep! was heard again apparently from among her skirts, and she too sprang to her feet and shook herself with a downward glance at them and a little nervous laugh. She was near her father, and he drew her to his knee, saying softly, "Don't be alarmed, darling, for you know there is really nothing there."

"Walter, can't you hunt up that chick?" asked Edward, looking gravely at his little brother. "Think how bad it would be for the poor little thing if somebody should accidentally tramp upon it."

"Why, I shan't need to hunt it!" exclaimed Walter. As the "Peep, peep, peep!" seemed to come from his pocket, he thrust his hand into it and sprang to his feet as he spoke; but at that instant a loud and furious barking just around the corner of the veranda attracted every one's attention.

"Down, sir, down!" cried a rough voice. "I'm neither thief nor tramp."

Another furious bark, then a low growl came in response, and baby Ned ran to his father with a frightened cry, "O papa, I's 'fraid doggie bite!"

"No, no, Neddie boy, papa won't let him harm his baby," the captain said, taking the little trembler in his arms, while Grace still kept close at his side.

The barking suddenly ceased, nor was the rough voice heard again, and Walter, running to the corner whence the sounds had proceeded, announced with a merry laugh that neither man nor dog was in sight.

"The chicken and the bee seem to have gone too," he added as he came running back, "and there's the tea-bell."

With that all rose and repaired to the dining-room. There Marian was seated beside Lulu, the captain next, Grace on his other side, and Violet and her two little ones opposite them.

A blessing was asked and the plates were filled; then a lull in the conversation was broken by a rough voice saying in a sarcastic tone, "Now ef you folks was as perlite and hospitable as we are out West, you'd invite this stranger to take a seat among ye and have a cup o' coffee and something to eat."

Almost every one looked startled and all eyes turned in the direction of the sounds, which seemed to come from behind Edward's chair.

" An invisible speaker, as might have been expected," laughed Violet.

" Show yourself, sir, take a seat at the table, and you shall be helped to all you wish of anything and everything upon it," said Edward, glancing about as if in search of the unexpected intruder.

" Show myself? Humph! keen-eyed you must be if you can't see a man o' my size," returned the voice.

" Perhaps so, sir," replied Edward, turning a knowing and amused look upon Cousin Ronald, " and I think I do see you very well. But have you been neglected? Your plate and cup look to me to be well filled."

" My plate and cup, sir?" exclaimed the voice in tones of indignant surprise. " Pray where are they?"

" Directly in front of Mr. Lilburn—or Cousin Ronald, as we, his relatives, are accustomed to call him."

" Why, laddie, I had thought you a hospitable host! and now would you rob me o' my supper which you have just bestowed upon me, and

3

give it to an unknown beggar-man?" exclaimed Mr. Lilburn in well-feigned astonishment and indignation.

"It does look very inhospitable, Ned; something to make me blush for my grandson," remarked Mr. Dinsmore, with a slight smile.

"Well, well," cried the rough voice, "it shall never be said of me that I set a family together by the ears. So I'll leave. Good-by."

A shuffling sound followed as of some one moving across the room in the direction of a door opening upon the veranda, then all was quiet. Every head turned in the direction of the sound, and as they ceased there was a general laugh; but the expression of Marian's countenance was perplexed and slightly alarmed.

"Who—what was it?" she asked with a slight tremble in her voice.

"Nothing alarming, my dear," replied Grandma Elsie in her sweet gentle tones; "we have a ventriloquist with us, that is all; and he not infrequently kindly amuses us with an exhibition of his skill."

"Ah! and it is Cousin Ronald?" Marian returned inquiringly and with a half-smiling glance into Mr. Lilburn's genial face.

Returning her smile, "Ah, little cousin, you seem to be as good at guessing as if you were a born Yankee," he said pleasantly.

"But it can hardly be that you are the only one," she said, as with sudden recollection. "Captain Raymond," turning to him, "I think I understand now about some puzzling things that occurred while you were at our house year before last. You too are a ventriloquist, are you not?"

"No, my dear girl, by no means," he replied.

"Then I have not, as I believed, found a solution of the mystery," she remarked reflectively; "but I think some one else who was there must have been a ventriloquist; for I know not how else to account for some things that occurred at Minersville when you were there: the beggar-boy and dog heard by four of us, but not seen; the voice speaking from the tree and the porch roof, that made Mr. Riggs so angry, and all that occurred on the evening of the Fourth, as you Americans call it."

"And that was doubtless the work of a ventriloquist," acknowledged the captain in a pleasant tone, "but I cannot claim any talent in that line."

"Then who could it have been?" she said with a puzzled look. "Ah! perhaps the English gentleman or his son. I remember they were often there conversing with you and Master Max."

Captain Raymond did not think it necessary

to reply to that remark, and other subjects of conversation were presently introduced. At the conclusion of the meal all repaired to the veranda or the grounds, and Cousin Ronald drew Marian aside for a little private chat.

"Tell me about your brother, lass," he said. "Is he happy? suited with his employment, think you?"

Marian hesitated for an instant, and then said frankly: "Poor Sandy longs for a good education, sir, but is willing to work hard and long for the means to pay his way in school and college."

"He is a good, industrious lad?"

"Never a better one, sir; he did all in his power to make himself useful and helpful to our dear mother and to me. He is as industrious and painstaking a lad as ever was seen. I am proud indeed of my brother—the only one of my mother's children, besides myself, that is left."

"Ah, he should have, must have help," said Cousin Ronald, leaning meditatively on his gold-headed cane. "Marian, lass," turning inquiringly to her, "he wouldna refuse it frae his own auld kinsman?"

"O Cousin Ronald, could you—have you it in your kind heart to help him to it? Bless you for it, sir! It would be the making of the dear lad. And should it please the Lord to spare his life I am very sure you may trust him to repay every cent of your outlay for him!" Marian cried with starting tears, and clasping her hands in an ecstasy of joy.

"Indeed could I and will I, lass," said the old gentleman, taking note-book and pencil from his pocket. "Give me his address and I will write to him to-night."

He wrote it down at Marian's dictation, then, restoring book and pencil to his pocket, "Now tell me of the dear mother, lassie," he said in low, feeling tones. "She loved the Lord, served him, and died trusting in his atoning blood?"

"She did, she did, sir!" sobbed the bereaved girl. "It was an awful sorrowful life she led from the time that cruel Mormon missionary deceived and cajoled my father into belief in the wicked doctrines and practices of that faith —so contrary to the teachings of God's own holy word—but she trusted in Jesus and at the last was full of joy that she was about to leave this world to dwell forever with him in that blessed land where sin and sorrow never enter. It was a terrible loss to me, but not for worlds would I bring her back, hard, hard though it be to live without her dear love and companionship."

"Yes, dear lass, but life is short, and if you trust in the Lord and his righteousness, you and she will spend a blessed eternity together at his right hand. But I will leave for the present," he added, "for evidently Cousin Elsie is watching for an opportunity to have a bit of private chat with you also."

With that the old gentleman rose and moved away and their lovely lady hostess took his place by Marian's side. She talked to the young girl in the kindliest manner, saying that she must let her be as a mother to her now while she was so young as to need a mother's loving care. "And you must let us, your own relatives, provide all needful things for you until you are educated and fitted to take care of yourself; which we will endeavor to do, remembering that all we have is the Lord's, intrusted to us to be used in his service, a part of which is helping others to fit themselves for usefulness."

"O cousin, how kind, how kind you and all these new-found relatives are!" exclaimed the young girl with emotion. "I cannot deny that I am too proud to—to enjoy, as perhaps I ought—being under such obligations; but I will and do accept it, hoping that my heavenly Father will some day enable me to repay—not the kindness, that could never be done—but the moneyed part of the obligation."

"That is right, dear girl," Elsie said, pressing tenderly the hand she had taken into hers, "and to begin with, I want to see that you are provided with clothing as good and abundant as have the other young members of our family connection. To-morrow Cousin Ronald and I, and one or more of my daughters, expect to go to the city and make purchases for you, and you shall accompany us and let your own taste and judgment be used in the selection of dresses and other needed articles, or stay behind and trust to our taste, as you may prefer. However, you need not decide that question to-night. The captain and Violet insist that you shall go back to Woodburn with them, and we will call at an early hour in the morning to hear what your decision is and take you with us, if you care to go."

"Dear Cousin Elsie, I don't know how to thank you!" Marian exclaimed with emotion; "you, and indeed all these new-found relatives, are so wonderfully kind to me; one who has not the shadow of a claim upon them."

"No, that is a mistake of yours, dear girl," Elsie returned. "The Bible bids us—those to whom God has given more or less of this world's goods—' that they do good, that they be rich in good works, ready to distribute, willing to communicate; laying up in store for themselves a good foundation against the time to come, that they may lay hold on eternal life.' But I will not detain you longer, for I would have you enjoy the company of our dear young folks to the full."

"I enjoy it greatly, but not more than your own, dear, sweet cousin," returned the young girl, gazing into Grandma Elsie's beautiful eyes with her own full of grateful, happy tears.

"You have enjoyed yourself to-day?" Grandma Elsie asked in tones of tender solicitude.

"Oh, very, very much!" was the quick, earnest rejoinder. "I never before had just such a day in all my life; though my mother used to tell me of similar ones in hers, for her near kith and kin were richer and of higher station than my father's—and were ill-pleased that she married him," she ended with a sigh.

"She married for love, I suppose?" Elsie said inquiringly.

"Yes," sighed Marian, "for love; but, as time proved, far more than half the love was on her side—unless it may be that love may turn to that which is little better than hatred."

"Ah, was it so bad as that?" Elsie asked with a grieved look into the sad eyes of her young relative. "If so, one cannot blame you if you have well-nigh ceased to love one so heartless as he has shown himself to be."

"Jesus said, ' By their fruits ye shall know them,' and such are the fruits of Mormonism," returned Marian; "the fruits brought forth in the lives of those who follow its hellish teachings. Is that too hard a word, cousin? It teaches lying, polygamy, assassination—their unscriptural, horrible blood-atonement doctrine —not one of which is to be found anywhere in God's own holy word. Oh, I thank the Lord that I have escaped out of their hands!"

"You well may, and I am very thankful for you, my poor, dear cousin," Elsie returned in tones of heartfelt sympathy.

But just then Rosie came and asked if Marian could not be spared to take part in some games the young people were about to begin.

An hour later the Woodburn carriage was in waiting at the veranda steps, and the captain and his party entered it and were driven home.

On their arrival there Gracie and the little ones went directly to bed, and while Violet was engaged in attendance upon them, the captain, Lulu, and Marian had the veranda to themselves.

"Here, Marian, take this big rocking-chair," said Lulu, drawing one forward, "and give me your hat. I'm going to hang mine on the rack in the hall, and may just as well take yours too; and papa's," holding out her hand for his, which he gave her with an approving smile as he seated himself upon a settee near the chair she had given Marian.

The next minute she was with them again, nestling close to his side, her arm around his neck, his about her waist, her eyes gazing up with ardent affection into his while her pretty little white hand stroked his face lovingly and toyed with his beard.

He was talking to Marian and hardly showed consciousness of Lulu's caresses except that he stroked her hair, patted her cheek, and pressed his lips absently once or twice to it or her forehead.

Marian's eyes filled at the sight, and she had much ado to keep her voice steady while answering his queries in regard to the growth and prosperity of Minersville, its schools, churches, and public works.

"Ah, what bliss to have such a father—so dear and kind!" was the thought in her heart. She expressed that thought to Lulu when they bade good-night after going upstairs.

"Indeed it is!" was Lulu's earnest rejoinder, "and I wish yours and all fathers were like mine. He isn't foolishly indulgent; all his children know they must yield ready and cheerful obedience whenever he gives an order, but it is always so evidently for our good, and so pleasantly spoken, unless we are showing ourselves wilful and stubborn, that it is not at all hard for any but a very bad, contrary child—such I have sometimes been, I'm ashamed to own—to obey."

"How blessed you are, Lulu!" sighed Marian. "But," she added with a look of surprise, "you did not bid him good-night, and I could not help wondering at the omission."

"Ah, that was because he will come presently to my room for just a few minutes' chat and a good-night kiss," Lulu said with a joyous smile. "Mamma, my own mother, used to do it, but she is gone now, and to our great joy papa takes her place in that. I would not miss it for anything; so good-night and pleasant dreams, for I must go."

"Good-night, you dear, sweet girl," Marian said, folding her arms about Lulu for an instant, and kissing her with warmth of affection. "I love you, and my now sainted mother loved you too. But oh, what would I not give for such a father as yours!"

## CHAPTER IV.

"WELL, how many of you would like to go to the city to-day?" the captain asked in pleasant tones the next morning at the breakfast-table. "You, my dear?" looking at Violet.

"No, thank you, sir, I think not, as I have a number of matters to attend to at home and will not be needed to assist in the shopping, as mamma and Sister Elsie are both going; probably Evelyn also, as some dresses are to be bought for her."

"You will go, Marian?" he said inquiringly, turning to her as he spoke. "You will want to exercise your own taste and judgment in the selection of articles of dress; at least so I presume, as such is the case with my eldest daughter," he concluded with a smiling glance at Lulu. "And she, I dare say, wants to be of the party."

"If you are going, papa," Lulu replied; "otherwise I'd rather stay at home, if I may."

"You may do exactly as you please, go or stay; so may Gracie."

"But you don't say whether you are going or not, papa."

"I shall stay at home, as there are some matters for me to attend to, perhaps nearly as important as those which will keep my wife at home," he said in a playful tone, turning toward her again as he spoke.

"I am not sorry to hear it, my dear," Violet responded.

"And I don't want to go," said Grace. "I never do like to go to the city without my father to take care of me," with an affectionate look up into his face. "Besides, I've promised to help Elsie arrange her doll-house and make some new clothes for her dollies."

"Ah? and of course promises must be kept; but as you do not want to go without papa you will not feel it a hardship, I hope, to keep yours to your little sisters."

"But I wouldn't want Gracie to stay at home if she wanted to go," said little Elsie; "no indeed I wouldn't, papa."

"No, my dear baby girl is not so selfish as that, I am sure," he returned with a loving look into the rosy, dimpled face. "But I feel quite sure Gracie does not want to go."

"And somehow papa always knows what we want, Elsie," Grace said with a contented little laugh.

"And as you will have Grandma Elsie, Aunt Elsie, Rosie and Evelyn along to help you select your dresses and other things, you won't miss me if I stay at home, Marian," said Lulu. "I want to get out our school-books—Gracie's and mine—and arrange our desks ready for school; for papa says we are to begin lessons again to-morrow."

"I shall miss you, I know," Marian answered with a smile; "but of course it is by no means necessary that you should go, and I should be sorry to be a hindrance to you."

Half an hour later the carriages from Ion and Fairview were seen coming up the drive. The Raymonds and their guest were all on the veranda, watching for them, Marian ready dressed for the little jaunt.

"Well, here we are!" called out a cheery voice as the foremost vehicle drew up in front of the veranda. "How many of you are going with us?"

"Only one—our young guest," the captain replied, handing Marian in as he spoke. Cousin Ronald, Grandma Elsie, and her daughter Rosie were its occupants, and each gave Marian an affectionate morning greeting. Then Violet stepped forward for a moment's chat with her mother, in which Rosie and the captain joined; thus leaving Marian and Mr. Lilburn the opportunity for a bit of private chat of their own.

"Lassie," he said with a kindly smile, "dinna forget that you are a sort o' adopted child o' my ain, and that I hae a father's right to at least help provide you wi' a' things needful," slipping a roll of bank-notes into her hand.

"Oh," she exclaimed, half under her breath and with starting tears, "how good and generous you are to me! I never had half as much in all my life."

"Why, my bairnie, you have na counted it yet!" he exclaimed with a low, gleeful laugh.

"No, sir; but such a roll—so many bills!"

He laughed again. "It's clear enough, lass, that you've had small acquaintance wi' bank-notes. One alone may be worth a thousand o' another denomination. There are twenty there —ten tens and ten fives."

"A hundred and fifty dollars! Oh, how much! I feel myself a woman of wealth. But what can I ever do to show my gratitude?" she said low and tremulously, happy, grateful tears shining in her eyes.

Then good-mornings were exchanged and the carriage drove on.

Toward evening Marian returned with what was to her an astonishing wealth of lovely apparel. She had a great dislike of mourning,

but had chosen quiet colors, such as met with
Grandma Elsie's cordial approval. Her purchases came to Woodburn in the carriage with
her; she took great delight in showing them to
Violet and the little girls, and they scarcely less
in looking at them.

"Now," said Violet, "we will get several persons to work to-morrow on your dresses and have
them ready as soon as possible for your wearing.
I am delighted with your choice, and feel sure
everything you have bought will prove very be-
coming."

"Oh, how good you are to me, dear Cousin
Vi!" exclaimed Marian with feeling. "But I
do think that after so much has been done for
me, to make up my dresses myself is the least
that ought to be asked of me."

"No, no, Marian," said the captain, "that
would never do. I could not think of allowing
it, because it would keep you so long out of the
school-room."

"Ah, my dear, it is easy to see that you are
in haste to get her where she will be subject
to your control," exclaimed Violet laughingly.
"Ah, Lu, don't look so indignant! that was
but a jest—a sorry one perhaps—for I appreciate
the kindness of your father's motives fully as
much, I think, as any one else can."

"Ah, I fear my dear eldest daughter is but a

silly little girl as regards her father and the respect paid him by others," remarked the captain, laying a hand affectionately upon Lulu's shoulder as she stood by his side.

"I'm afraid I am, papa," she returned, coloring and smiling rather shamefacedly, "but I just can't bear to have even Mamma Vi talk as if you weren't quite perfect." At that the captain laughed.

"It would never do coming from a daughter," he said, "but is entirely excusable in a wife."

"Thank you, sir," laughed Vi, "I quite appreciate the privilege you accord me."

"I'm afraid it is time for me to go to my room and make myself neat for tea," said Marian, pulling out a pretty little watch; at which Lulu and Grace cried, "How lovely!"

"Yes; it is another of Cousin Ronald's gifts; something I had hardly ever dared to hope to possess. Was it not good and kind in him to give it to me?"

Then she told of the roll of bank-notes he had put into her hand that morning, and that the price of the watch did not come out of that.

It was handed about from one to another, admired by all, then returned to its owner, who immediately gathered up a number of her packages and, with Lulu and a servant carrying the rest, hastened to her room.

4

The two girls came down again presently in answer to the tea-bell.

It was the usual tempting meal to which they sat down, simple but daintily prepared, daintily served, and made all the more palatable and enjoyable by cheerful chat in which even the little ones were allowed a share.

On leaving the table Marian was taken by Lulu and Grace to see the school-room.

"Oh, what a lovely room! what beautiful desks and comfortable-looking chairs!" she exclaimed. "And with your dear father for teacher it must be only a pleasure, a great pleasure, to study here!"

"So Lu and I think," said Grace, "though I must own that there are times when I'm a little lazy."

"I too," said Lulu, "oftener than Gracie, I think; but though papa is always very patient and kind, he insists that if we are well the lessons must be learned."

"I am sure that is kind," said Marian; "a good education is so, so valuable—better than wealth, because not so easily lost."

"And for other reasons quite as well worth considering," added a manly voice behind them, and turning in its direction they found Captain Raymond standing near.

Marian's look was inquiring and he went on:

"Knowledge of the right kind brings more real pleasure into one's life than can be found in wealth, fits one for greater usefulness, and is, as you just remarked, not so easily lost."

"Very true, sir," Marian responded thoughtfully, "and if you help me to gain that you will be a benefactor indeed."

"I am disposed to do all I can to help you, my good girl," he said in a kindly tone; "and I think your companionship with Lulu in her studies will so interest and spur her on that I shall feel more than repaid for the slight addition to my labor."

"Papa," asked Grace thoughtfully, "doesn't it say somewhere in the Bible that it is better to get wisdom than gold?"

"Yes; in Proverbs Solomon exclaims, 'How much better is it to get wisdom than gold! and to get understanding rather to be chosen than silver; and knowledge rather than choice gold. For wisdom is better than rubies; and all the things that may be desired are not to be compared to it.' But doubtless he there refers to heavenly wisdom—a saving faith in the Lord Jesus Christ, who is the wisdom by which God established the heavens and founded the earth."

"When am I to begin school, captain?" asked Marian presently.

"I think I will let you off until next week, if

you wish it," he replied in a playful tone; "or, as I go to Annapolis for a day or two early the week after, perhaps you may as well delay beginning your studies until my return."

"O Marian, don't! do begin next Monday," urged Lulu. "I do so want to have you with us in the school-room and for you to find out what a good and kind teacher papa is."

"His eldest daughter being the judge," remarked the captain with an amused look.

"And his second daughter being of exactly the same opinion," added Grace, slipping a hand into his as she stood close at his side.

He pressed it affectionately, then, still holding it fast, proposed that they should return to the veranda where they had been sitting before the call to the tea-table.

He led the way with Grace, the others following, and presently the four were seated there, Grace close to her father on one side, Lulu on the other, and Marian near at hand.

"O Marian, do say you will begin lessons next Monday," urged Lulu again. "I'm perfectly sure your dresses can be fitted by that time, and if there is any fitting not done, it can be attended to out of school hours; or papa will let you go for a little; for he's always reasonable and kind; if it is his own little girl that says so," she concluded with a roguish look up into her father's face.

"Ah, Marian, if you are wise you will not put too much faith in the opinion of one who evidently looks at the person under discussion through rose-colored glasses," remarked the captain in a gravely warning tone.

"It seems to be the way with every one who knows you, sir," laughed Marian; "so I will be on my guard till I have learned more of you through my own observation."

"And do you mean to wait till you have satisfied yourself upon that point before you venture to become one of his pupils?" queried Lulu.

"It would not be waiting very long, as I am already satisfied that Captain Raymond is to be trusted; for I have had a report of his teaching and government from both Rosie and Evelyn; a most favorable one from each," Marian said in reply.

"And of course they wouldn't be as likely to prove partial judges as his own daughters who love him so dearly," remarked Grace, with her arm about her father's neck, her eyes gazing fondly into his.

"I think I shall venture," returned Marian. "My intention is to be careful to keep rules and to work very hard at the lessons; so doing

I cannot think I shall run much risk of punishment. The worst he could inflict (expelling me) would only—I was going to say, leave me where it found me; it would be worse than that, though—real disgrace and disappointment; but I don't intend ever to be so idle, mischievous, or rebellious as to bring it on myself."

"I have not the slightest fear that you will," said the captain, "and I think too that I know you pretty thoroughly since the weeks spent in the same house with you in Minersville."

"And do you intend then to begin on Monday?" queried Lulu with a look of joyous expectancy.

"Yes, indeed; if nothing happens to prevent. I do not want to lose any time, for I wish to be able to earn my own living as soon as possible."

"Why, what a very independent young woman you seem to be, Cousin Marian!" laughed a sweet girlish voice close at hand, and Violet tripped lightly from the doorway to a chair which her husband, hastily putting Grace from his knee, drew forward for her use.

"Thank you, my dear," she said, taking possession. "You are intending to become one of my husband's pupils, Marian?"

"He has invited me, and I have thankfully accepted," Marian replied. "I think it a most kind and generous offer."

" I entirely agree with you in that opinion," Violet returned with a look of ardent, admiring affection up into her husband's face, " but can assure you that kindness and generosity are nothing new for him."

" Ah, I knew that much about him before he left Minersville," returned Marian. " Many there can testify to his great kindness and generosity."

Just then a carriage was seen coming up the drive and the captain rose with a sigh of relief to meet and welcome his guests, who proved to be callers from one of the neighboring plantations.

The next morning, while the other young folks resumed the duties of the school-room, Marian was, with Alma's assistance, busied with planning, cutting, and fitting the new dresses. Each had heard something of the other's story. Alma had many questions to ask about life among the Mormons, and the more she heard from Marian in reply, the more did she rejoice in the narrow escape of herself and sister from their toils.

The moment they were dismissed from the school-room, Rosie, Evelyn, and Lulu came in search of Marian. Rosie had some news to tell.

" Mamma had a letter this morning from my brothers Harold and Herbert, begging and entreating her to come to the commencement at Princeton. I suppose you all know that they are to graduate, and they think they must have mamma there; to enjoy their triumph, I presume," she added laughingly.

"And will she go?" asked Marian.

"I think she will," replied Rosie, "and that grandpa and grandma will go with her. They both have relatives in and about Philadelphia and will take the opportunity to visit them too."

"On which side is the relationship with Cousin Elsie?" asked Marian, with a look of interest.

"Oh, they are none of them her mother's relatives," said Rosie. "But grandpa's half-sister —Aunt Adelaide—married a brother of Grandma Rose; so she and her children are related to both sides of our house, and Grandma Rose has other brothers and sisters in that neighborhood besides her old father and mother. So she likes to visit there frequently."

"And they of course must always be delighted to have her with them; such a sweet, lovely lady as Cousin Elsie is!"

"But she will go first to Max's commencement, won't she, Rosie? I mean the commencement at the Naval Academy at Annapolis," said Lulu.

"She says she wants and intends to," replied

Rosie; "that is, if she is well enough, and she certainly seems very well indeed just now."

"I am so glad of it!" exclaimed Lulu. "We are all going, in the *Dolphin*, if nothing happens to prevent, and I hope all of you girls will be with us. It is so lovely there and I think we are likely to have a delightful time."

"It will all be new to you, Marian," observed Rosie pleasantly.

"Oh, I do not expect to make one of the party," returned Marian quickly and with a blush.

"Papa said you were to go if you wanted to," said Lulu, "and I am sure you would if you could realize what a delightful trip it will be."

"I thank both you and your father, Lulu, very much indeed," Marian returned with a blush and a smile, "but I have little or nothing fit to wear at such a place and in such company, and it would be entirely impossible for me to get ready in season."

"Yes, I suppose so," said Lulu, looking somewhat disappointed; "but there will probably be other times when you can go," she added, brightening up.

At that moment Grace looked in at the door with an announcement: "Grandma Elsie, Grandpa Dinsmore, and Cousin Ronald are in the veranda, talking with papa and mamma."

"And are we invited to join the conference?" queried Rosie in a merry, jesting tone.

"I don't think it's a secret conference," replied Grace, "and I suppose we can all join it if we want to."

"I should like to do so if I could leave my work," Marian said, "but I must stay and attend to it unless they say I am wanted for some particular reason."

"In that case we'll let you know, Marian," said Lulu as she and the others hastened from the room together.

They found the older people arranging plans for attending the Annapolis and Princeton commencements; it was already decided that to the first all would go from Woodburn and Ion who cared to, some of them by rail, the others in the *Dolphin*, then Mr. and Mrs. Dinsmore and Grandma Elsie to the other; and also, before returning, they would spend some weeks in visiting friends and relatives in and about Philadelphia.

The young folks listened quietly but with intense interest, now and then exchanging glances which told plainly how delighted they were with the prospect of having a share in the expedition to Annapolis; even Grace, who usually thought home the most desirable place for her, being no exception.

She presently stole to her father's side, slipped her hand into his, and looked up into his face with a bright, glad smile.

"I am to go too, papa?" she asked in a low tone, meant only for his ear.

"Unless you prefer to stay at home, daughter," he said, putting an arm around her and drawing her closer to him, smoothing her hair with the other hand and smiling fondly down into the fair young face.

"Oh, no, sir! I want to go, 'specially as Mamma Vi and Elsie and baby Ned will all go along; and we'll be in the *Dolphin* and not in the tiresome cars."

"Yes, I think the *Dolphin* is far more comfortable than the cars, and I trust the little trip will prove very enjoyable to us all," he replied, by no means ill-pleased that his little girl was so happy in the prospect.

# CHAPTER V.

TIME moved on swiftly enough to the older people, busily engaged in preparations for the contemplated trip to Annapolis, yet with rather laggard step to the younger ones, who were in haste to experience its pleasures and excitements. But in the performance of school duties they one and all acquitted themselves quite to the captain's satisfaction; even excitable Lulu finding it not nearly so difficult to concentrate her thoughts upon the business in hand as it had been when first her father began to act as tutor to his children. Also Marian's companionship in her lessons during the second week was an assistance to renewed and increased interest in them.

But at length the appointed day for the sailing of the *Dolphin* came. Marian adhered to her decision to remain behind, attending to the preparation of her summer wardrobe, but the others, all in good health and spirits, were ready and eager for the trip.

The weather was charming, making their drive to the city delightful; the rest of the short journey on board the *Dolphin*—which they found awaiting them at the wharf and in the most beautiful order, everything about her deck and above and below looking spick and span as though she had but just come from the hands of her builders and decorators.

They arrived the day before that on which the graduating exercises were to be held, dropping anchor in the Severn just as the afternoon artillery drill began. They witnessed it from the deck and could see that Max was a prominent figure therein. He seemed to go into it most enthusiastically, and they all, his father especially, watched his every movement with pride and delight.

He had purposely left the lad in ignorance of the exact time of the expected arrival, and Max discovered the near vicinity of the *Dolphin* only when the exercises had come to an end. At the same instant a message from the commandant reached him, giving permission for him to go aboard the yacht and remain there until half-past nine that evening, and the *Dolphin's* row-boat was seen to leave her side with the captain in it.

In a very few moments more Max was on the deck of the yacht, surrounded by those nearest and dearest to him, his father looking on with beaming eyes while they crowded around the lad with their joyful and affectionate greetings.

"Now, Max, sit down here among us and give a full account of yourself, your doings and experiences since we saw you last," said Grandma Elsie with an affectionate smile into the bright young face, and making room for him by her side as she spoke.

Max gave his father an inquiring look, and receiving an approving nod in reply, took the seat and did his best to answer satisfactorily the questions which were showered upon him from all sides: queries as to the progress he was making in his studies, great-gun exercise, field artillery, infantry tactics, etc., and in regard to various other matters.

But a joyous bark suddenly interrupted the talk, and Max's dog Prince bounded into the midst of the group, raised himself upon his hind legs, put his fore-paws on his young master's shoulders, his tail wagging fast with delight, and tried to lick Max's face.

"Why, hello, Prince, I'm glad to see you, old fellow!" cried the lad, patting and stroking him, but avoiding the caress. "There, that will do; you try to kiss harder and longer than any other of my friends."

"P'raps that's because I love you harder," Prince seemed to say. "And it's longer since

I saw you last. The captain never invited me to come along before."

"He didn't?" laughed Max. "Well, I don't believe you asked him; but I'm right glad to see you here at last. Also to find you haven't forgotten how to talk."

"No, my young master, but it's the first time I've done anything in that line since you left me at Woodburn."

By this time everybody was laughing.

"Oh, Max, who is making Prince talk—you or Cousin Ronald?" asked Lulu.

"See if you can't find out for yourself, Lu," laughed Max. "Suppose you ask Prince; surely he should know."

"Well, I'll try it," she returned merrily. "Prince, who helped you to do that talking just now?"

"Why, who helps you to talk, Miss Lu?" came promptly in return, apparently from the dog's lips.

"Oh, I don't need any help in that line," she returned laughingly, "and never have since I first learned how in my babyhood."

"Do you never tire of talking, Miss Lu?" The query seemed to come from Prince's lips as he looked up gravely into her face.

"No, I can't say that I do," she laughed. "Do you?"

"I am oftener tired of not being able to express my thoughts and feelings," was the reply. Then the call to tea put an end to the conversation for the time.

Prince followed the others to the table and when all were seated laid himself down at Max's feet. There he lay looking up into the lad's face, and when the plates had been filled a low whine seemed to say he too would be glad to have a share of the savory viands.

"Just wait a bit, old fellow, and your turn will come," said Max. "You never starve where my father is master, I'm sure."

"No, that's true enough; but it is not always so easy to wait when one's hungry and sees other folks with plates heaped with savory victuals right before them. Why shouldn't dogs be helped at once as well as men, women, and children?"

Prince's tail swept the floor and his hungry eyes looked up wistfully into those of his young master as the words seemed to come from his lips.

"Well done, Prince! such efforts at speech ought to be duly rewarded," remarked the captain gravely; then he directed a servant to take the dog out and feed him well.

"What is the programme for this evening?" asked Violet; "a trip up the river again? '

"If you and the others wish it, my dear," replied her husband, to whom her query seemed to be addressed. "I had thought, however, of going down the river and bay, as we went up on our last visit here. We will put it to the vote of those present. I am quite indifferent personally as to which course we pursue." It soon appeared that the majority were in favor of moving toward the bay, and on leaving the table the captain issued his orders, the *Dolphin* weighed anchor, and the wind being favorable, they sailed down the river and out into the bay.

"Annapolis is a very old town, is it not, Brother Levis?" asked Walter.

"Yes," was the reply; "it was founded by the Puritans under Captain William Clayborne. He first settled over yonder on Kent Island in 1631, but was expelled from there—he and his adherents—in 1638, for refusing to acknowledge allegiance to the newly established government of Lord Baltimore. In 1642 some Puritans, expelled from Virginia for non-conformity, settled where now stands Annapolis, founded a town there and called it Providence. In 1691 it became the capital of the State and the name was changed to Annapolis."

"You have gone farther back in its history than you ever did in telling us about it before, papa," remarked Lulu.

"Ah? how far back did I go before?" he asked pleasantly.

"To the time when they heard of the resistance to the passing of the Stamp Act by the people of Massachusetts, sir," she replied. "Don't you remember that when we were sailing from Newport to Annapolis, to bring Max here to enter the Academy, we young folks all gathered round you, just as we have to-night, and asked for revolutionary happenings in Maryland?"

"Ah, yes, I do remember it now, though it was nearly a year ago," he returned, looking with a humorous smile down into her eyes.

"Why, just think," exclaimed Max, "the town was then more than a hundred years old. What a venerable old place it is now!"

"Ah, no wonder you grow manly so fast, young sir, living in such a grand old place," remarked a strange voice apparently coming from the rear of the little party seated pretty close together on the deck.

Naturally every head turned in the direction of the sound, but the speaker was not to be seen.

"Who and where are you, sir?" queried the captain. "Step forward and take a seat with the rest of us."

"Thank you, sir; but I do not want to intrude. You must excuse me for coming aboard, but I wanted a sail and thought my weight wouldn't retard the boat. I'll pay for my passage if you say so."

The speaker continued invisible, though every word was distinctly heard.

"Then do so by giving us a sight of your face," returned Captain Raymond.

"It is not covered, sir, and you are all welcome to look your fill," was the reply.

"Where is de mans, papa?" asked little Ned, gazing wonderingly about.

"Sitting in Cousin Ronald's chair, I think," replied his father, smoothing the curls of the little prattler, who was seated upon his knee.

"No, papa, dat Tousin Ronald."

"Well, then, perhaps it was Brother Max."

"No, papa, Bruver Maxie not talk dat way. Does oo, Maxie?"

"I think not, Neddie boy," returned Max, smiling on the baby boy and giving his round rosy cheek an affectionate pat.

"No, no, little chap, I'm not Brother Max," said the voice, sounding somewhat farther away than before, "or any such callow chicken, but a full-grown man."

"Ah, ha, I know now that it is Cousin Ronald," laughed Lulu, "for Max would never call himself a callow chicken."

"I shouldn't think Cousin Ronald would call

him so either," said Grace in a hurt tone; "chickens are cowardly and I'm sure Max is not."

"Better not be too sure, but wait till you see him tried, miss," said a squeaky little voice, coming seemingly from another part of the vessel.

"Now that's you, Max, I know, because it is the very same voice we heard at Minersville on the evening of the glorious Fourth," remarked Lulu with a merry laugh.

Max neither acknowledged nor denied that she was right. Looking up and catching sight of the Stars and Stripes floating from the masthead, "O Lu," he asked, "do you know who invented our flag—'old glory,' as we love to call her?"

"Why, no; who did?"

"A little woman named Betty Ross, a Philadelphia Quakeress. She had a great deal of taste, was particularly fond of red, white, and blue, and adorned many of the apartments we read of in colonial history; the halls of Congress, the governor's reception-room in Philadelphia, among others. She was acquainted with a number of the great men of the time— Morris, Franklin, Rittenhouse, Adams, and best and greatest of all—our Washington. And she had a brother-in-law, Colonel Ross, who was a gallant American officer in the Revolutionary War.

"On the 14th of June, 1777, Congress was considering about a design for a national flag, and it was at once proposed that Betsy Ross should be requested to design one. The committee asked Colonel Ross, Dr. Franklin, and Robert Morris to call upon her. They went and General Washington with them. Mrs. Ross consented, drew the design, and made the first American flag with her own hands. General Washington had showed her a rough design which she said was wrong—the stars having six corners when the right number was but five. She said she didn't know whether she could make the flag, but would try; which, as I have just said, she did, and succeeded so well that Congress was satisfied with it; and it was the first star-spangled banner that ever floated on the breeze."

"There was an eagle on that flag, Max, was there not?" asked the captain as the lad paused in his story.

"Yes, sir; a spread eagle with the thirteen stars in a circle of rays of glory. It is said that many eminent men visited Mrs. Ross' shop while she was at work on the flag and were deeply interested in it."

"Well," remarked Lulu thoughtfully, "if

that flag was flung to the breeze in June of 1777, it is a mistake for people to say that the rough flag made and floated at Fort Schuyler the next fall was the first."

"Quite true," said her father, "though probably they—the makers of the Fort Schuyler flag—had not heard of the other and believed theirs to be the first. It is stated that Washington had displayed at Cambridge, Massachusetts, on January 2d, 1776, what might be called the original of our present banner. It had thirteen stripes of red and white with a St. Andrew cross instead of the stars."

"Was there not another called the rattlesnake flag?" asked Rosie.

"Yes, in two forms: in one the figure was left complete, and under it were the words, 'Don't tread on me.' In the other the snake was in thirteen pieces—in some cases with thirteen rattles—and the legend was 'Join or die.'"

The captain paused a moment, then went on: "I was reading lately an account taken from an English paper of what was probably the first floating of the American flag in British waters. It was on February 3d, 1783, that the ship *Bedford*, a Massachusetts vessel commanded by Captain Moore, passed Gravesend, and on the 6th she was reported at the custom-house. The Lords of Council and the Commissioners of the

Customs held a consultation, because of the many acts of Parliament still in force against the ' rebels ' of America—as our British cousins were wont to style us—before allowing her regular entry. She was American built, manned wholly by American seamen, and belonged to Nantucket, Massachusetts.

"The article goes on to say she carried the ' rebel ' colors and was the first to display the ' rebellious stripes of America in any British port.'

"But before that the Stars and Stripes had appeared on British soil. A noted philanthropist and sturdy patriot of Philadelphia, named Elkannah Watson, had at the close of the Revolutionary War received four hundred guineas as a wager, and on the same day was dining with the painter Copley, whom he engaged to paint his portrait for the sum of money just obtained from the wager. The portrait was all finished but the background, which they had agreed should represent a ship bearing to America the news of the acknowledgment by the British government of our independence—the Stars and Stripes floating from her gaff and gilded by the rays of the rising sun was still wanting, the painter considering it imprudent to put it there at that time, as his gallery was the resort of royalty and the nobility. Watson speaks of

' the glorious 5th of December, 1782,' on which he and Copley listened to the speech of the king in which he formally received and recognized the United States of America as one of the nations of the earth.   After that Watson went home with the artist to dinner; but before sitting down to the table Copley finished his picture, inviting his company to be present in his studio while 'with a bold hand, master touch, and American heart' he attached to the ship the Stars and Stripes."

"That was displaying what the British had called the rebel colors very promptly upon the king's acknowledgment, and very near his palace," remarked Mr. Dinsmore with a smile of grim satisfaction.

"Yes; doubtless a bitter pill for his majesty to swallow," laughed Rosie.

"Well, he needn't have had it to swallow if he hadn't been so tyrannical and obstinate," remarked Walter.   "I remember that Bancroft says, ' The American struggle was avowedly a war in defence of the common rights of mankind.' "

"That is very true, Walter," returned his grandfather.   "They—the leading men of the time—were a noble band of patriots and lovers of their kind.   We have a right to be proud of them."

"And I am proud of them, sir," returned the lad, his cheeks glowing and his eyes sparkling.

"That's right, my little man; everybody should love his country and feel proud of all its people who resist tyranny and stand up boldly for the principle that 'all men are created equal; that they are endowed by their Creator with certain inalienable rights; that among these are life, liberty, and the pursuit of happiness,'" said a strange voice which seemed to come from their rear.

Every one turned to see the speaker; then finding he was not visible, laughed pleasantly.

"I am glad to learn that you are so well acquainted with our glorious Declaration of Independence, Cousin Ronald, and seem to appreciate it so highly," remarked Grandma Elsie, with a smiling look into the pleasant face of her kinsman.

"Ah, indeed, cousin! are you entirely sure that I am deserving of that compliment?" queried Mr. Lilburn gravely.

"Quite sure," she returned. "I could hardly have quoted it so correctly myself."

"But was that my voice, cousin?" he asked.

"One of your voices, I have no doubt," she replied laughingly.

"Mr. Lilburn," said Max, "I have been telling some of my comrades of your ventriloquial powers and they are extremely desirous to witness their exercise. Will you not kindly gratify them while here?"

"Why, laddie, I am hardly more capable in that line than yourself," laughed the old gentleman.

"But you, sir, are not under authority as I am and so liable to be called to account for your doings."

"Eh! perhaps not. Well, well, we will be on the lookout for opportunities, you and I. I own I am not averse to gratifying the young folks when I can do so without displeasing their elders."

## CHAPTER VI.

A MOMENTARY silence following upon Mr. Lilburn's remark was broken by a question from Grace. "We are away out in the bay now, aren't we, papa?" she asked.

"Yes, daughter, and must turn presently, for Max's leave of absence will be over by the time I can take him back to the Academy."

"But I may hope to be with you all again to-morrow and the next day, when the graduating exercises are over, may I not, papa?" asked Max.

"I think so; provided you keep out of scrapes," his father replied, laying a hand affectionately on the lad's shoulder as he spoke, for Max was now close to his side. "And one evening or the other—both if you like—you may bring some of your mates with you, and perhaps Cousin Ronald and you yourself may be able to entertain them with some exertion of your ventriloquial powers."

"Oh, thank you, papa," said Max delightedly; "nothing could be better. Cousin Ronald will, I dare say, make great sport for them, and perhaps I could do a little myself. But whom

75

shall I invite? I am very sure any of them would be delighted to come."

"I leave the selection to you, my son," replied the captain. "Choose any whom you think the right sort of company for yourself and us and likely to enjoy being here."

"Thank you, sir. How many shall I ask?"

"Well, my boy, as we are not expecting to keep them over night, six or eight would not, I think, be more than we can accommodate comfortably."

"And that will be as many as I care to ask at one time," Max said with satisfaction. "Hunt will be glad to come, I know, and he's a nice fellow."

"You'll want to ask those who are anxious to make Cousin Ronald's acquaintance, I presume," said his father.

"Yes, sir, some of them; if I asked all it would include my whole class besides a good many belonging to the others," laughed Max.

"Very well," said his father, "you know about how many we can accommodate, and I leave the selection to you, feeling quite sure that my boy will prefer those of good character for his intimate associates."

"Yes, indeed, papa, and I thank you very much for trusting me."

The *Dolphin* was presently at her wharf

again and the good-nights had to be said; but, expecting to have Max with them the next day and the day after, even his sisters were not sad over the parting, while the lad himself was jubilant in the pleasant prospect of entertaining his boy friends and comrades on board the yacht. He hurried to his room and filled up the few remaining minutes of the half-hour allowed for recreation before retiring for the night, with giving Hunt, his room-mate, a glowing account of his visit to his father's vessel, and extending the invitation for the next afternoon and evening, which Hunt accepted promptly and with evident delight.

The next day was spent by most of the party from Woodburn and Ion in walks and drives about the city and its vicinity, varied by some attendance upon the exercises at the Naval Academy; but before tea-time all were on board the yacht again, where they were presently joined by Max and his party.

The lads were all evidently in high good humor and on the tiptoe of expectation, knowing that they were about to make the acquaintance of the ventriloquist of whose tricks Max had told them many an exciting tale.

The introductions were over, all had been comfortably seated, and some few minutes spent in desultory chat, when Hunt, addressing

Max, who happened to be his nearest neighbor, asked in a low tone when the show was to beign.

Max smiled and there was a roguish twinkle in his eyes, while at the same instant a voice spoke from behind Hunt, "I say, young fellers in blue, what's brung so many o' ye aboard here to oncet?"

There was a simultaneous sudden start and turning of faces and eyes in the direction from which the sounds had come. But the speaker seemed to have instantly disappeared, and the momentary start was followed by a general hearty laugh.

"The captain's invitation," replied Hunt, while his eyes and those of the other lads turned upon Mr. Lilburn.

"All right then," responded the same voice, seeming now to come from a more distant part of the deck; "he owns the yacht and kin ask anybody he's mind to."

"Of course," said Hunt, "and it was very kind in him to ask us. Did he invite you also, sir?"

"None o' your business," came in reply in a surly tone.

"Truly a gentlemanly reply," laughed Hunt. "One might readily infer from it that you were not here by invitation."

"What do you mean by that, sir?" demanded the invisible speaker, in loud, angry tones.

"That your conduct and speech proclaim you no gentleman, while Captain Raymond is decidedly such."

"Come, come, friends, don't let us have any quarrelling here," came in pleasant tones from the other side of the vessel.

"Now who are you, sir? This isn't your fight, and you'd better keep out of it," returned the first voice; "your interference will be asked for when it's wanted."

The lads exchanged looks of surprise and one of them asked:

"Are you doing it all, Mr. Lilburn, sir?"

"Ah ha, ah ha! um h'm, ah ha! so you think 'twas I, young sirs!" exclaimed the old gentleman in pretended astonishment. "And why so? Did the voices issue from my lips?"

"I cannot assert positively that they did, sir," returned Hunt, "but they seemed to come from an invisible speaker, and knowing you to be a ventriloquist, we think it can all be accounted for in that way."

"Knowing me to be a ventriloquist, eh, laddie! And may I ask how you came by that same knowledge?"

"Through our friend, a naval cadet like ourselves, Mr. Max Raymond, sir. Do not be vexed with him for telling us. It has excited our admiration and desire to make your acquaintance."

"Ah, Master Max, so you have been letting these young gentlemen into my secrets?" Mr. Lilburn said, turning toward Max in pretended wrath.

"Yes, sir," replied Max in cheerful tones, "and the more you show them of your skill in that line the better they will be pleased."

Just then Max's dog Prince joined the group, wagging his tail and lifting joyful eyes to his young master's face.

"Ah, how d'ye do, Prince?" said Max, stroking and patting him. "Are you glad to see me here again?"

"Yes, sir, indeed I am," were the words that seemed to come in reply from the dog's lips; "and I wish you'd go back with us when we steam away in this vessel for home."

"Why, Prince, you talk well indeed for a dog," laughed Hunt, stroking and patting Prince's head.

At that instant there was a frightened cry, "Oh, sic' a fall as I shall hae!" followed instantly by a sound as of the plunge of a heavy body from the side of the vessel into the water.

All started to their feet, several of the men and boys shouting in tones of alarm, "A man overboard!" and Captain Raymond was about to issue an order for the launching of a boat, when a glance at Mr. Lilburn deterred him.

"No occasion, captain," laughed the old gentleman; "you could never find that poor unfortunate fellow."

"No, I presume not," returned the captain, echoing the laugh as he and the others reseated themselves.

"Huh! that's an old trick o' yours, old feller," cried the very same voice that had been heard behind Hunt's chair. "If I couldn't invent suthin' new I'd give up the business."

"So I think I shall—for to-night, at least," returned Cousin Ronald, but in a disguised voice that seemed to come from a distance.

Then Walter went to his side and whispered in his ear.

Mr. Lilburn smiled and seemed to assent, but at that instant the call to the supper-table put an end to the sport for the time.

There was some of the same sort of diversion at the table, however, a roast fowl resenting, with a loud squawk, the captain's attempt to carve it; Prince asking audibly for a share when the plates were filled, and the voice that had been heard talking on deck to the "young fellers in blue" preferring the same request.

These tricks, though old to the others, were

6

new to the cadets and caused a good deal of merriment; as did the buzzing bees, peeping chick, barking pups, and squealing pigs that seemed to have taken possession of the deck on their return thither.

At length these sounds were replied to by a loud and furious barking coming apparently from some remote part of the deck, and to which Prince immediately made response in kind, at the same time rushing away in search of the intruder.

"A pretty time you'll have finding that new-comer, Prince," Walter called after him.

But the words were hardly spoken when a third loud bark was heard coming apparently from yet another quarter, and Prince, repeating his, rushed in that direction; then three or four dogs seemed, from the sounds, to be barking, snarling, yelping as though a furious canine fight was in progress; though nothing could be seen of the combatants except the huge form of Prince as he searched in vain for the intruders of his race.

But the noise woke the little ones who had been put to bed in the cabin below, and a frightened wail from them brought a sudden hush, while Violet rose hastily and hurried down the companionway to sooth and reassure her darlings.

That put an end to the ventriloquial sport, and the remainder of the short time allowed for the visit of the cadets was spent in more quiet fashion, desultory talk and the singing of songs

They had been steaming down the river and bay and back again while they talked and sang; the wharf was reached shortly after nine o'clock and the lads returned safely and in good season to the Academy.

They one and all expressed themselves as highly delighted with their visit to the yacht and were very enthusiastic in their praises of the ladies; particularly Grandma Elsie and Violet, whom they pronounced the sweetest, most beautiful and charming women of their acquaintance.

They felt acquainted with them now, they said, for after Cousin Ronald and Max had ceased their ventriloquial performances they had had an opportunity to talk with the ladies as well as to listen to the music with which they kindly entertained them.

"I have always thought you a fortunate fellow, Max," remarked Hunt as they were preparing for bed, "and since seeing the yacht and that young grandmother and stepmother of yours, I am more fully convinced of it than ever. I was just going to say I wondered at so young and lovely a creature as Mrs. Raymond marrying a man with a son of your age, and two other children not young enough to be her own; but remembering what your father is—so handsome, noble-looking, so entirely everything any one could ask or desire—I do not wonder at all at her choice. In fact, she may consider herself quite as fortunate as he in the selection of a partner for life."

"So I think," responded Max heartily; "for to me it seems that my father's superior—indeed, I might say his equal—is not to be found anywhere; and I know Mamma Vi would agree with me. I have never known him speak a hasty, sharp, or unkind word to her, and he waits upon her as gallantly as he could possibly have done in the days of their courtship.

"As to the children left him by my own mother—my father promised before marrying Mamma Vi that she should have no care or trouble in regard to them; that he would take all that upon himself; and so he has and does; when he has been at home with us we have always felt that he did. So it is no wonder if we esteem him the dearest and best of fathers; while Mamma Vi is hardly a mother, but more like an older sister to us—unless it may be to Grace, the youngest of our set."

Here the signal for the extinguishing of lights and retiring to rest put a stop to the conversation, and in a very few minutes the lads were soundly sleeping.

One more day was spent at Annapolis by the Woodburn and Ion people; then an early evening train carried the latter party northward, and an hour later the *Dolphin* steamed away with the others.

Walter and Rosie would have been glad to go with their mother, but she and their grandfather had decided that it would be better for them to continue their studies for the present, as the time for the summer holidays was not distant; and like the well-trained, affectionate children they were, they submitted cheerfully to her decision, determining to make the best possible use of their opportunity for education.

Their mother expected to be at home again in a fortnight, or sooner, but they had rarely been separated from her for even a day, and the parting was a trial to both. They bore it bravely, however, slept well that night on board the yacht, and rose the next morning apparently as gay and light-hearted as their wont.

They were both early on deck, where they found the captain and Lulu together, watching the sun just peeping above the waves far away to the east.

"Good-morning, brother Levis and Lu," called Rosie, tripping across the deck in their direction. "I thought Walter and I were extremely early, but there is no use in anybody trying to get ahead of you two in early rising."

"Good-morning, little sister," responded the captain, turning toward her with his pleasant smile. "There was no occasion for you and Walter to leave your couches quite so early this morning, or for either of you to do so. I believe Lulu and I happen to be of the kind who need a little less sleep than do many others."

"Yes," said Lulu, with a loving look up into her father's face, "papa would let me sleep another hour if I wanted to, but I almost always wake early and do so enjoy the little time that it gives me with him before the others are up and wanting some of his attention for themselves."

"I don't wonder," said Walter, "for I like to be with mamma the first thing in the morning dearly well."

The boy's voice sounded a little choked at the last, and he dropped his eyes lest the others should see the sudden tears welling up in them.

The captain laid a kind hand on the lad's shoulder. "If our dear mother is awake now she is doubtless thinking lovingly of her youngest son and asking God to bless and keep him from all evil. You may hope to see her again in about two weeks, which will pass very quickly, and in the mean time let us think of all we can

accomplish to give her pleasure on her return,"
he said. "Shall we not, little brother?"

"Yes, oh, yes, sir!" replied Walter, looking
up brightly into the pleasant face above him.
"I mean to study hard and keep all your rules
carefully, so that you can give her a good account of my conduct and recitations. Oh,
there's the sun just entirely up out of the
water! What a grand sight it is!"

"One that I never weary of," said Captain
Raymond in a meditative tone and gazing east-
ward upon the newly risen luminary as he spoke.
"It reminds me of Him who is called the Sun
of righteousness, because He is the quickener,
comforter, and illuminator of His people."

"Papa, didn't people in the Old Testament
times worship the sun?" asked Lulu.

"Yes," replied her father, "it is thought
that the Moloch of the Ammonites, the Chem-
osh of the Moabites, and the Baal of the Phœni-
cians was the sun."

"I remember that the Israelites also sometimes wandered away from the true God and worshipped Baal," remarked Walter; "that Elijah
the prophet slew of Baal's prophets four hundred and fifty men; and that afterward Jehu
filled a house with Baal's prophets, priests, and
worshippers and had them all put to death."

"Yes," the captain said, "that was in accordance with the command of God given in Deuter-onomy, seventeenth chapter. I will read it to you," he added, taking a small Bible from his pocket. Turning to the passage he read:

"If there be found among you, within any of thy gates which the Lord thy God giveth thee, man or woman that hath wrought wickedness in the sight of the Lord thy God, in transgress-ing his covenant, and hath gone and served other gods, and worshipped them, either the sun or moon, or any of the host of heaven, which I have not commanded, and it be told thee and thou hast heard of it, and inquired diligently, and behold it be true, and the thing certain that such abomination is wrought in Israel; then shalt thou bring forth that man or that woman, which have committed that wicked thing, unto thy gates, even that man or that woman, and shalt stone them with stones till they die."

"That gives us some insight into God's hatred of idolatry," remarked the captain, closing the book.

"Yes, sir," said Rosie. "I am reading Deu-teronomy just now in my regular course. I was at the fourth chapter yesterday, and was struck with what is said there about the worship of images. Won't you turn to the chapter and read it aloud to us, brother Levis?"

"Certainly," he replied, opening the book again and turning to the passage to which she had referred. Beginning at the fifteenth verse he read:

"Take ye therefore good heed unto yourselves; for ye saw no similitude on the day that the Lord spake unto you in Horeb out of the midst of the fire; lest ye corrupt yourselves, and make you a graven image, the similitude of any figure, the likeness of male or female, the likeness of any beast that is on the earth, the likeness of any winged fowl that flieth in the air, the likeness of anything that creepeth on the ground, the likeness of any fish that is in the waters beneath the earth: and lest thou lift up thine eyes unto heaven, and when thou seest the sun and the moon, and the stars, even all the host of heaven, shouldest be driven to worship them, and serve them, which the Lord thy God hath divided unto all nations under the whole heaven. . . . Take heed unto yourselves, lest ye forget the covenant of the Lord your God, which he made with you, and make you a graven image, or the likeness of anything which the Lord thy God hath forbidden thee. For the Lord thy God is a consuming fire, even a jealous God. When thou shalt beget children and children's children, and ye shall have remained long in the land, and shall corrupt yourselves, and make a graven image or the likeness of anything, and shall do evil in the sight of the Lord thy God, to provoke him to anger; I call heaven and earth to witness against you this day, that ye shall soon utterly perish from off the land whereunto ye go over Jordan to possess it; ye shall not prolong your days upon it but shall utterly be destroyed."

"I would have you all notice," the captain said, again closing the book and speaking with earnestness, "how plainly and repeatedly God forbids the worship of images, likenesses, or of any of the creatures or things he hath made; how repeatedly and expressly he commands us to worship him and him alone."

"Ah, no wonder that the popish priests forbid their people to read the Bible for themselves," said Rosie, "for from it they would soon learn the wickedness of bowing down to and worshipping images, crucifixes, and pictures."

"Yes," replied Captain Raymond, "and I would far sooner lay my children in the grave, dearly, dearly as I love them, than to see them bowing down to images and pictures; serving 'gods the work of men's hands, wood and stone, which neither see, nor hear, nor eat, nor smell.' How precious is the promise that follows in that same chapter, 'But if from thence thou shalt seek the Lord thy God, thou shalt find

him, if thou seek him with all thy heart and
with all thy soul. When thou art in tribula-
tion and all these things are come upon thee,
even in the latter days, if thou turn to the Lord
thy God, and shalt be obedient unto his voice
(for the Lord thy God is a merciful God), he
will not forsake thee, neither destroy thee nor
forget the covenant of thy fathers which he
sware unto them.'

"Verily I believe that we of the Anglo-Saxon
nations are the literal descendants of Abraham,
Isaac, and Jacob—God's own chosen people—so
that we have the strongest claim to these precious promises; but let us never forget that they
are ours only as we fulfil the prescribed condi-
tions; without true repentance and true faith
we shall no more be saved than those of other
nations who do not seek the Lord while he may
be found and call upon him while he is near."

Just then little feet came pit-pat across the
deck, a sweet child voice calling out, "Good-
morning, papa, dear papa, I's an early bird too,
isn't I?"

Quite an early bird for such a wee one," the
captain answered, holding out his arms, then
as she sprang into them clasping her close and
kissing her fondly again and again; the next
moment doing the same by Grace, who had followed closely in Elsie's wake.

The rest of their party soon joined them, then came breakfast and family worship; after those an hour or two on deck; then the vessel steamed into the harbor, her passengers landed and found the Woodburn carriage in waiting, with those from Fairview and Ion; Edward and Zoe with their twin babies in the one, Lester and Elsie Leland, with their two boys, in the other.

Affectionate greetings were exchanged, and soon all were on their homeward way. They found the drive delightful, the roads in excellent condition, gardens, fields, and woods arrayed in all the luxuriant verdure and bloom of the month of roses.

The children in the Woodburn carriage seemed full of mirth and jollity.

"Really I don't believe any one of you is sorry to be nearing home again," their father said, regarding them with eyes full of paternal affection and pleasure in their evident enjoyment.

"No, indeed, papa," cried the little girls in chorus, while Ned said in his baby fashion: "I's blad, papa; my home is a dood place; me 'ikes it, me does."

"Mamma echoes that sentiment, baby boy," laughed Violet, giving the little fellow a hug. "There's no place like home; home with dear papa and all the dear sisters in it."

"Bruver Maxie too?" returned the little fellow in a tone between inquiry and assertion.

"Ah, no; not just now," Violet answered with a slight sigh, for she loved Max and missed his cheery presence in the house.

"Ah, here we are!" the captain exclaimed presently as the carriage turned into the driveway.

"And everything is looking oh, so lovely!" cried Lulu, clapping her hands with delight. "And there is Marian on the veranda, waiting for us."

The other two carriages were not far behind. It had been arranged that all should dine together at Woodburn; so they also turned in at the gates, and presently all had alighted and were one after the other warmly greeting Marian. She was glad to learn that Mr. Lilburn had been invited to make Woodburn his home for some weeks and had accepted the invitation, so that she would see much of him for a time at least and become better acquainted. He had been so kind to her that she felt already a warm affection for him as a near and dear relative.

## CHAPTER VII.

MR. AND MRS. DINSMORE and Mrs. Travilla reached Philadelphia safely, without accident or detention, spent a few days with their relatives there, then, being urgently invited to pay a visit to the family of their cousin Donald Keith —the brother of our old friend Mildred, wife of Dr. Landreth, of Pleasant Plains, and father of Mary Keith, with whom Edward and Violet spent some time in a cottage at Ocean Beach in the summer after the death of their father— they did so.

About six years had passed since then. Some of Mary's younger brothers and sisters had grown up and married, so that her burdens were much lightened, but she herself was still single and at home in her father's house.

Time seemed to have stood still with her. They found her the same bright, cheery girl, looking scarcely older than she had looked six years ago.

She was delighted to see again these relatives whom she had met and learned to love during that ever-to-be-remembered summer in the cottage by the sea, and very glad to hear all they had to tell of the cousins who had helped to make enjoyable her effort at housekeeping then and there. She had many questions to ask about them and the little ones, and expressed an ardent desire to see them all again, to which her cousin Elsie replied: "We are expecting to return home in a fortnight, or a little sooner, and will be glad to take you with us if you will go, Mary; will you not, dear girl?"

"Cousin Elsie, how very kind in you!" exclaimed Mary, both tone and look full of delight. "But," she added with a doubtful glance at her mother, "I fear I could hardly be spared from home."

"Now don't be so conceited, Mary Keith," laughed that lady, with a mischievous glance into the flushed, eager face of her eldest daughter. "I think I am quite capable of keeping house and attending to all family affairs without a particle of aid from you. So if Cousin Elsie wants you and you want to go, I advise you to set to work at once at your preparations—putting your wardrobe in perfect order and adding to it whatever may be needed. Oh, you needn't look doubtful and troubled! Your father has been greatly prospered of late, and I know will not feel any necessity or inclination to deny anything desirable to the good daughter who has been a very great help and comfort to him and me through years of toil and struggle."

Mary was affected even to tears. "O mother, how good and kind in you to say all that!" she faltered. "I have done no more than my duty—hardly even so much, I fear."

"Possibly your father and I may be as capable of judging of that as yourself," returned Mrs. Keith in the same tone of careless gayety she had used before; "and we think—for we were talking the matter over only the other day —that our eldest daughter deserves and needs some weeks of recreation this summer. We were discussing the comparative merits of sea and mountain air, but finally decided to leave the selection to yourself; and now doubtless Cousin Elsie's kind invitation will decide you in favor of a trip to the South, even in spite of its climate being less suitable for the warm weather than our own."

"It will be a change for her, at all events," Elsie said, "and when we come North again, as we expect to do in a few weeks, we may, I think, hope to return her to you rested and invigorated. Or, still better, we will hope to take her, with your consent, with us to the sea-shore for a good rest there before returning her to you."

Mrs. Keith and Mary returned warm thanks for this second invitation, but it was not at that time definitely settled whether or not it could or would be finally accepted.

"Ah, mother dear, I see now why you insisted this spring on my buying and having made up more and handsomer dresses than ever I had in one season before," Mary said presently with an affectionate look and smile into Mrs. Keith's pleasant and still comely face.

"Yes, it is always wise to be ready for sudden emergencies," returned the mother playfully, "and I think you can easily be ready for a visit to Ion by the time Cousin Elsie will be on her way home from Princeton."

"Our plan is to start for home in about a week," Elsie said, "as the commencement will be over by that time, and my boys, Harold and Herbert, ready to accompany us."

"You are making us a very short visit, Cousin Elsie," remarked Mrs. Keith. "I hope when you come up North again you will piece it out with a much longer one."

"Thank you," returned Elsie. "I should enjoy doing so, and perhaps may be able to; but our plans for the season are not arranged."

Then turning to Mary, "Our party is to pass through Philadelphia on our return after the commencement. Can you not arrange to meet us there so that we may travel the rest of the way to Ion in company?"

7

"I think so," was the reply. "Can I not, mamma?"

"I see nothing to prevent," said her mother. "We will have you there in season if our cousins will let us know what train you are to meet."

Mr. Dinsmore came in at that moment, and with his good help the arrangements were presently satisfactorily completed.

To the great delight of Harold and Herbert, their grandfather and mother arrived safely in Princeton on the evening of the day before commencement.

The young men, though looking somewhat overworked, yet seemed in good health and good spirits. They had passed successfully through their examination and the next day were graduated with high honors.

Both grandfather and mother showed by their looks, manner, and words of commendation and congratulation that they were highly gratified and not a little proud of their bright, intelligent, industrious lads.

"And now, my sons, I suppose you are quite ready for home?" their grandfather said when the congratulations were over.

"Almost ready to start for it, grandpa," Harold replied with a joyous laugh. Then turning to his mother, "Mamma, I have a request to make, and I do not think you or grandpa will object to its being granted."

"Not if it is anything reasonable, my dear boy," she returned. "Are you desirous to invite some friend to accompany us to Ion?"

"Ah, mother mine," he laughed, "you certainly are good at guessing. Yes, I should like to give a warm invitation from grandpa, you, and ourselves to a classmate whose home is closed at present, his parents being in Europe for the health of his mother, who is a sad invalid. William Croly is his name—Will we call him—and he is as good, bright, and lovable a fellow as could be found anywhere."

"He is indeed, mamma," said Herbert. "I esteem him as highly as Harold does."

"Then I think he will be a very welcome guest at Ion," Mrs. Travilla returned with a look of inquiry at her father, as if she would consult his wishes as well as her own and those of her sons.

"I should ask him by all means," said Mr. Dinsmore. "I judge from the recommendation just given that he will prove a pleasant guest; besides, the Bible bids us 'use hospitality without grudging.'"

"And that is one thing I am sure you and mother love to do, grandpa," returned Herbert, giving a look of affectionate admiration to first one, then the other.

"Yes, it is a great pleasure, therefore hardly meritorious," his grandfather said with a smile.

"Then I may bring Croly and introduce him, may I not?" asked Harold.

A ready assent was given in reply. Harold hurried away and presently returned, bringing with him a young man who had a very pleasant, bright face and refined, gentlemanly manners.

Mr. Dinsmore and his daughter gave him a pleasant greeting and kindly shake of the hand as Harold introduced him, and after a little a cordial invitation to accompany them on their return to Ion and remain until they should all come North again for the summer.

Croly was evidently delighted with the invitation, and it did not take much urging to induce him to accept it.

That evening they all journeyed to Philadelphia, where they were joined by Mrs. Dinsmore and Mary Keith, and the next morning the whole party started southward, a pleasant, jovial company.

They met with no accident or detention, and were greeted with the warmest of welcomes on their arrival at Ion at an early hour on the second day.

They took some hours of rest and sleep, then were able to enjoy the family gathering which had been planned by Elsie's sons and daughters to celebrate the safe return of their loved mother and grandparents from their visit to the North and the home-coming of the young graduates.

The children and young people were included in the invitation, and not a single one failed to be present. From Woodburn, the Oaks, Pinegrove, Roselands, the Laurels, and Fairview they came, forming of themselves alone a goodly company, full of mirth and jollity, which was in no way checked by any of their elders, with whom they remained for a time, hanging about those who had been absent from home, particularly Grandma Elsie, and next to her the young uncles, who had been away so long that they seemed almost as strangers to the very little ones; pleasant and attractive strangers, however, inclined to make much of their little nieces and nephews, a business in which their college friend, Will Croly, took an active part.

Almost every one presently forsook the rooms and verandas to sit beneath the trees or wander here and there about the beautiful, well-kept grounds, visiting the gardens, hot-houses, and the lovely little lakelet.

A handsome rowboat was there and the young men invited the older girls to take a row around the pretty little sheet of water. Marian McAlpine, Evelyn Leland, Rosie Travilla, and the two

Dinsmore girls from the Oaks accepted, but Lulu Raymond, who was with them, regretfully declined, saying she knew papa would be displeased if she went without his knowledge and consent.

"Why, Lu, you are growing remarkably good and obedient," laughed Sidney Dinsmore.

"For which we should all honor her," said Harold. "The captain is one of the best and kindest of fathers and his requirements are never unreasonable."

"Oh, of course not," laughed Sidney; "only I'm glad he hasn't the care of me and control of my actions."

"I'm glad that he has of me and mine," returned Lulu rather hotly as the boat pushed out into the water, leaving her standing alone on the shore gazing wistfully after it. "How delightful it looks," she sighed to herself. "I wish I had thought of the possibility of such an invitation and got papa's permission beforehand."

"You did right, little girl, and I am very sure that when your papa hears of it he will commend you in a way that will give you far more pleasure than the row could have done if taken without his permission," said a voice from behind her, and turning to look for the speaker, she found Mr. Lilburn close at hand.

"Thank you, sir," she replied with a pleasant smile. "I wanted badly to go, yet I know I couldn't have enjoyed it without papa's permission."

"I should hope not indeed," returned the old gentleman.

"Oh, Mr. Lilburn," cried Lulu, struck with a sudden thought, "there are several in our company here this afternoon who know nothing of your ventriloquial powers. Can't you think of some way of using them that will puzzle the strangers and furnish amusement for us all?"

"Suppose we consider that question—you and I," he returned with a smile. "Have you any suggestion to make?"

"How would it do to make them hear trumpets or bugles or something of that kind in the woods near by, as you did to the Ku Klux years ago?" she asked in eager tones, adding: "Grandma Elsie has told us the story of their attack on this place when Mamma Vi was quite a little girl."

"Ah, yes, I remember," he said with a slight smile. "Let us sit down here," leading her to a rustic seat near at hand, "and I will see what I can do to excite the curiosity of the strangers."

"Oh, I'm glad now I was left behind!" Lulu exclaimed as she took the offered seat and turned an excited, expectant face toward her companion.

For a minute or more he seemed buried in thought, then suddenly the clear notes of a bugle seemed to come from behind a clump of trees a few rods distant from where they sat.

Lulu was startled for an instant and turned in that direction, half expecting to catch a glimpse of the bugler. Then she laughed and clapped her hands softly.

"Oh, that's lovely!" she said. "They'll be sure there's somebody there and wonder who it can be. Yes, see how they are turning their heads in that direction."

"Can you see the expression o' ony o' their countenances, bit lassie? I canna, for my eyes are growing old."

"Yes, sir. I can see that Miss Keith looks startled and astonished and seems to be questioning Uncle Harold, and that Mr. Croly is laughing and trying his best to catch a peep at the trumpeter. The others I think look as if they are trying to keep from laughing. I dare say they see you here, sir, and can guess what it means. Oh, there's our Prince! He seems to be in search of the trumpeter."

Even as Lulu spoke she was startled by another bugle-blast seemingly directly behind them, or from the branches of the tree under which they sat.

"Oh!" she exclaimed, turning quickly to

look behind her; then with a merry laugh, "I wasn't expecting your bugler to come so very near, sir."

But the concluding words were almost drowned in Prince's loud bark as he came bounding toward them, evidently in search of the intruding bugler.

"Find him, Prince, find him as fast as you can and teach him not to intrude into the Ion grounds," laughed Lulu.

But the bugler's notes had already died away and Prince's bark changed to a low growl as he searched for him here and there, but vainly.

"So you have a bugler on the estate, eh?" Croly was saying, with an inquiring glance at Harold. "One of your darkies, I presume? They are a musical race, I know."

"They are," Harold replied with unmoved countenance.

"I thought the notes musical and pleasant," observed Miss Keith, "but they do not seem to have taken the fancy of your dog."

"Prince—a fine fellow, by the way—is not our dog, but belongs to Max Raymond," said Herbert. "No, he does not seem to fancy the intruder, whoever he may be."

"Hark!" cried Rosie, "the bugler is at it again."

"And this time it is a Scotch air," remarked

Mary Keith. "How soft and sweet it sounds! But it comes from quite another quarter; yet I do not know how the bugler can have changed his position so entirely without any of us catching sight of him as he went."

"It does seem odd," said Croly. But his words were nearly drowned in the loud bark of Prince as he rushed in the new direction, with evident intent to oust the intruder this time. His effort was, however, as complete a failure as the former one. The notes of the bugle died softly away, the dog sniffed about the tree from which they had seemed to come, but finally gave it up and trotted away in the direction of the house. "Point out that bugler to me when we come across him, won't you, Harold?"

"Really I never knew that we had a bugler among our servants," returned Harold evasively.

"Nor I," said Herbert. "But," taking out his watch, "it is nearing tea-time, and as we are likely to find plenty of opportunities for this kind of sport, I think we had better now return to the house."

No one objected, the boat was immediately headed for the wharf, and all had presently landed and were sauntering along by the way that they had come, Mr. Lilburn and Lulu accompanying them.

## CHAPTER VIII.

"WHAT in the world has become of that bugler?" queried Croly, peering among the trees and shrubs."

"Were you wanting to speak to him, Mr. Croly?" asked Rosie, gravely but with some difficulty restraining a desire to laugh.

"No, not particularly, but I have a slight curiosity to see him and ask for another specimen or so of his skill."

"He seems to be skilful in making his disappearance, doesn't he?" laughed Rosie.

"He does, and I suppose I shall have to give up the hope of making his acquaintance," returned Croly. "But it is really singular that no one of us has been able to get sight of him."

"It is indeed," assented Mary Keith. "I have been watching closely, but without obtaining so much as a glimpse of him."

"Well, cousin, don't despair; perhaps it will be better luck next time," Herbert said laughingly. "Ah, we are just in time, for I see they are setting the tables beneath the trees."

"Oh, that's good," cried Lulu. "I think it

is such good fun to eat out of doors." Then aside to Mr. Lilburn, " O Cousin Ronald, can't you do some of those things you did at Cousin Betty's wedding? It would be such fun."

" Wait and see, bit lassie," the old gentleman returned with a smile.

Just then Walter came bounding to meet them. "I'm glad to see you," he said half breathlessly. "I've been hunting all around for you, because tea is nearly ready and Zoe was afraid you might not be here in season."

" Eh, laddie," laughed his brother Herbert, "so you forgot, did you, that we had appetites and watches?—the first to remind us of our need of food, the second to tell us when it was likely to be served."

" I thought it kinder to hunt you up than to trust to appetites and watches to bring you in good season to get everything at its best," returned Walter good-humoredly.

Then stepping close to Mr. Lilburn's side, he asked in an undertone, " Cousin Ronald, please won't you make some of the same kind of fun for us that you did at Cousin Betty's wedding?"

At that Mr. Lilburn laughed, saying: " Well, well, laddie, you and your niece here (you're Lulu's uncle, aren't you?) seem to be of one mind in regard to that matter. We'll see what can be done."

"Walter's niece!" laughed Lulu. "He's younger than I am and would be a little uncle for me."

"So I would," laughed Walter in turn, "but if your father is my brother I suppose you must be my niece, and you'd better mind what I say to you."

"I will—when it suits me," she replied in merry retort.

They were now nearing that part of the lawn where they had left the older members of the party and the little ones.

"Ah, I am glad to see you," said Zoe, coming forward to meet them, "for it is nearly time for the summons to tea."

"Yes; we hope we have not kept you waiting?" returned several voices.

"Oh, no," she replied cheerily, "you are just in good season. I heard your father inquiring where you were only a moment since, Lulu."

"Oh, did you, Aunt Zoe? Well, I'll tell him," replied Lulu, hurrying away in his direction, for she could see him seated under a tree at some little distance, with Mr. and Mrs. Dinsmore, Grandma Elsie, Mamma Vi, and several others. Lulu stole up behind him, put her arms round his neck, and laid her cheek to his.

"Ah!" he said, taking hold of the small white hands, drawing her around in front of him, and seating her on his knee, "where has this eldest daughter of mine been for the last hour or so?"

"Down by the lake with the older ones, papa," she replied, softly stroking his beard with one hand and smiling archly into the eyes gazing so fondly upon her. "I thought you were always willing that I should go about the grounds here without asking special permission."

"Yes, so I am, provided you do not go on the water without my knowledge and consent."

"I wanted to, but I didn't," was her reply. "You didn't think I would, papa, when you had forbidden me?"

"Certainly not, daughter. It would be a sad thing indeed if I could not trust you out of my sight."

Their conversation had been carried on in an undertone and the others were not listening, but chatting among themselves.

In the mean while Cousin Ronald had drawn Zoe aside and held a moment's low-toned conversation with her, which seemed to interest and amuse her. Then Edward joined them, Zoe seemed to repeat to him what the old gentleman had said, Edward responded with a smile, then the three separated, and the young host and hostess—the mother having resigned to them her duties in that line for the evening—proceeded to seat their guests at the tables, and servants appeared bearing the viands prepared for their entertainment.

Mary Keith, Marian McAlpine, and Will Croly were all three at one and the same table, Mr. Lilburn, Harold, Herbert, Rosie, and Evelyn Leland sharing it with them. The last two and the brothers exchanged furtive glances of amused expectancy. Mr. and Mrs. Dinsmore, Grandma Elsie, Walter, and the Raymonds occupied the next two; the rest of the company others not far distant.

Almost every one seemed in gay spirits and all were blessed with good appetites, the satisfying of which kept them very busy for a time, though not to the entire exclusion of mirthful chat and laughter.

But when the more substantial dishes had been duly discussed, carried away, and replaced by cakes, fruits, and ices, in a moment of comparative silence there came a sudden sound as of flapping of wings overhead, followed by a shrill call—

"Lu-lu! Polly wants a cake. It's supper-time and Polly hungry."

"Why, Polly, how did you get out and fly all the way here?" cried Lulu in astonishment, and looking up, as did almost every one else, among the branches overhead. "I didn't think you knew the way; and there is plenty for you to eat at home."

"Lu-lu! where are you? Polly's hungry. Polly wants a cup of coffee," came in return in what seemed evidently Polly's own shrill tones.

"Go home and get it, then," laughed Lulu. "You weren't invited here, and well-behaved people always wait to be asked before they go visiting."

"Polly's hungry. Poor old Polly—poor old soul!" came in response.

"Why, where is she?" queried Grace, peering up among the branches of the tree from which the sound seemed to come.

"I don't know," said Lulu. "I can't just see her, but she has a good hiding-place up there where the branches and leaves are so thick. But how she found her way here I can't think. Oh!" as she suddenly caught sight of Mr. Lilburn's face and noted the twinkle of fun in his eye.

"Perhaps you have given her too much liberty, Lulu," her father said in so grave a tone she was at loss to decide whether or not his suspicions too had been aroused.

"So you have a poll-parrot, Miss Lu? Quite a talker too," said Croly. "I should like to make her acquaintance. Can you not tempt her to come down?"

" I'll try to keep her at home after this, papa," said Lulu; " but shall I see if I can coax her to come down now?"

" You may if you choose," he answered with unmoved gravity.

" Tell her she can have a cup of coffee and anything else she wants if she will come," added Grandma Elsie, with a look of amusement.

So Lulu called, " Polly, Polly, come here and you shall have a cup of the nicest coffee and anything else you want."

Then for a minute or more everybody seemed to be looking and listening; but Polly neither answered nor showed herself, and at length baby Ned broke the silence with, " I 'spect Polly's done 'way to our house adain. She won't tum when Lu talls her."

" She seems to have taken her departure very suddenly," remarked Rosie. " Strange she should do so if she were really as hungry as she pretended."

" I don't b'lieve she was, Aunt Rosie," said little Elsie, " for nobody ever gets starved at our house, 'cause papa always buys plenty for everybody to eat."

" It's good food too, and well cooked," added Grace.

" I think that is all true, Mr. Croly, and I

8

hope you will come and see for yourself,' laughed Violet.

"Hush, hush, hush! you talk too much, Polly," came in a shrill scream apparently from the top of the tree; then in a coaxing, complaining tone, "Poor Polly's hungry! It's breakfast-time. Polly wants a biscuit. Polly wants a cup of coffee."

"Why, she's quite a talker. I'd really like to get a sight of her," said Croly, making a more determined effort than before to do so.

"Humph! savin' all your pity for hungry birds! Never a bit of it to give a starvin' human creeter," snarled a man's voice that seemed to come from a clump of bushes a yard or two in Croly's rear. Every head at once turned in that direction, but the speaker seemed invisible.

It was Grandma Elsie who replied: "There is abundance of food here, and I would have no one starve or suffer at all from hunger. Step up to the table and your wants shall be supplied."

"There is no empty seat at your table, ma'am," snarled the voice.

"True," she returned, "but there are abundance of seats near at hand, and you can carry your food to one of them when you have received it, and there sit and eat at your leisure."

"Why, where on earth is the fellow?" asked

Croly of Harold, speaking in an undertone. "I cannot catch so much as a glimpse of him."

"It really looks very mysterious," returned Harold, with difficulty repressing a smile. "What had better be done about it, do you think?"

"Surely that is for your mother to say," returned Croly; "but if I were in her place I should have the grounds thoroughly searched for that impudent fellow, who is probably a thieving tramp."

"Hardly, I think," said Harold, "for they are somewhat scarce hereabouts; at least, we seldom see one."

"Ah? then you are fortunate in that respect."

"But how odd that both bird and man should be invisible!" exclaimed Mary Keith. "I must own that I cannot understand it."

"No," remarked Herbert gravely; "there are many things happening in this world that we cannot understand."

"But it surprises me to see how easily you take all this. Now I should want to hunt him out and send him about his business before he does any mischief."

"Perhaps that might be the better plan," returned Harold. "Here, Prince," as Max's dog was seen slowly approaching, "hunt out

"But you know who it is?"

"Why do you think so, Miss Mary?"

"Something in your look and manner tells me that you know all about it; besides, you were on the shore while we in the boat heard the sounds of the bugle apparently coming from among the tree-tops."

"Really, now, Miss Mary, I don't see that all that proves anything against me," laughed Lulu. "Do you think it does, papa?"

"Not at all," replied her father. "A ventriloquist on the boat might, I think, make it seem to others that his voice came from among the tree-tops on the shore. But really, Mr. Croly," turning toward the young man as he spoke, "I do not see that you have any positive proof that there is a ventriloquist here."

"Why, sir, did we not hear a strange voice speaking apparently from yonder clump of bushes, and on examination find that there was no one there?"

"True; but who shall say it may not have been some one very nimble and fleet of foot who made his escape all too quickly to be caught?"

"Well, sir," returned Croly slowly and with meditative air, "I suppose that is just possible. Perhaps too the same fellow was the bugler whom we all heard but none of us could see."

"Edward," said Mr. Dinsmore gravely, "you

may as well have the premises searched for that
fellow; for one so adroit at suddenly disappear-
ing from sight might readily enter the house
and carry off valuables."

"Yes, sir; I'll see that he does not," Edward
replied with equal gravity, but carefully ab-
staining from an exchange of glances with Mr.
Lilburn.

"Take care that he doesn't steal your parrot,
Lu," said Zoe. "She's worth stealing, and as
she is such a good talker I'd be loath to lose
her if she were mine."

"Indeed so should I," exclaimed Lulu. "I
wouldn't part with her for a great deal; especially as she was a present from papa."

"We will be careful not to leave her here
when we go home to-night," said the captain.

"I hope you are not afraid to trust her with
us, captain," said Zoe. "I assure you we would
be good to her, and I dare say she would prove
a great amusement to my babies."

"I have not a doubt that you would treat
her well, sister Zoe," replied the captain, "and
if Lulu is inclined to lend her for a few days, I
shall not object."

"Then I'll not take any trouble to hunt her
up when we're ready to go home," said Lulu.

All had now satisfied their appetites, the
tables were presently forsaken, and the company

gathered in groups here and there under the
trees, some amusing themselves in playing
games, others with conversation; but it had
been a long June day, and before the sun had
fairly set most of them were on their homeward way; for Mr. and Mrs. Dinsmore and
Grandma Elsie, hardly rested after their journey, began to look weary.   Mr. Lilburn, at the
urgent invitation of the captain and Violet,
returned with them to Woodburn to complete
his visit there, which they said had not been
half long enough.   Marian too was with them,
so that they were quite a little party.

Grace and the little ones went directly to
bed on reaching home, but the elder ones passed
a pleasant hour or two on the veranda before
returning.

## CHAPTER IX.

"MOTHER dear," Harold said, as he kissed her good-night on that first evening at home after their return from Princeton, "Herbert and I are decidedly hungry for one of the good old talks with you; but you are too weary to-night. May we come to you early in the morning for the dear old half-hour of Bible study and private talk before breakfast?"

"I shall be very glad to have you do so, my dear boys," she replied, regarding them with eyes beaming with mother love and pride. "I have been looking forward with longing for the confidential talks with my boys which have always been so sweet to me; especially in regard to your plans for future usefulness as workers in the Master's vineyard."

"Yes, mamma, that is one of the principal matters about which we wish to consult you—our best, dearest, wisest earthly friend," said Herbert, lifting her hand to his lips; "for who so wise, so loving, or so desirous to help each of us to use time and talents in a way to make them most helpful in the Master's service?"

"I cannot lay claim to any great amount of wisdom, my dear boys," Mrs. Travilla returned with a smile, "but am certain no one can love you better or feel a greater desire than I to see you earnest, efficient workers for Christ. I want very much to talk over with you your plans for the future, and think there could be no better time for doing so than that early morning hour when we shall be more secure from interruption than at almost any other. Now good-night, and may you rest sweetly and peacefully on this first night at home after your long absence."

"May you also, dear mother, precious little mother," said Harold, passing an arm about her waist, and smiling down with ardent affection into her still fair, sweet face. "I remember that I used to look up at your beautiful face, regarding you as a protector, but I feel that now I am yours—old enough and strong enough to defend you should any be so base as to attempt to do you harm."

"Ah, my dear boy, fortunately no one has, I think, any such desire," she said, returning his smile; "yet it is very pleasant to feel that I have so many strong young arms to support and shield me. 'Twas very pleasant in former years to be the protector of my little ones, and it is not less pleasant now to find them so ready to re-

turn my love and care. But now go to your
beds, for you need rest and sleep to keep you
in condition for the arduous duty of which we
have just been speaking," she added with playful look and tone.

"How early can we come without disturbing
you, mother mine?" asked Herbert, snatching
another kiss as Harold released her from his
arms.

"At seven, if that is not too early," she replied. "Rosie and Walter are usually with me
about half-past seven, and the breakfast-hour
is eight."

They were at her dressing-room door the next
morning exactly at the hour named, and found
her ready to receive them. A pleasant chat
followed, the lads telling her freely of their
plans and desires in regard to their life-work;
for diligent workers they intended to be. Harold still clung to his early choice of the medical
profession, and Herbert, as devotedly attached
to him as ever, and thinking he would not
prefer any other employment, had decided to
study medicine also unless his mother should
disapprove.

"No," she said when he asked the question,
"I shall be glad to have you together; so unless
you, Herbert, have a stronger inclination for
some other employment I shall be more than

satisfied to see you a physician; always provided you are a good one," she added playfully. "Is it your wish, my sons, to return shortly to Philadelphia and pursue your medical studies there?"

"Not immediately, mother," Harold replied. "We were talking the matter over with Cousin Arthur last night, and he being willing to undertake the business of instructing us, our plan is to stay at home with you for some time, studying with him. That is, if you are satisfied to have us do so."

"Ah, I am much more than satisfied—most glad and thankful at the thought of again enjoying daily intercourse with these two dear sons who have been so long away from me during the greater part of the year. But just now you both need rest and recreation. You must have an outing somewhere for the next month or two, and I shall be glad to have you go with me to sea-shore or mountains—or both—and hope to bring you back refreshed and invigorated for your studies and such work for the Master as you may find in this neighborhood."

"Thank you, mother dear," returned Harold; "you have made out a programme that seems most inviting. I for one feel that rest and recreation for a time will be very enjoyable, and work afterward much more so than it could be at present."

"I also," said Herbert; "and it is certainly right to take rest when needed; for the Master himself said to his disciples, when they were weary, 'Come ye yourselves apart into a desert place, and rest awhile.'"

"Yes," assented his mother, "and we shall accomplish more in the end by taking needed rest; yet," with a smiling glance at Herbert, "we must be on our guard against too much self-indulgence in that line."

The young man colored and was silent for a moment, his face wearing a slightly mortified expression. "Mother dear," he said presently, "I hope I have, in a measure at least, overcome my natural inclination to indolence."

"My dear boy, I hope and believe so," she said in return, "else you could hardly have passed so good an examination as you did."

"Indeed, mother, he has been really a hard student," Harold said, "and I think will undoubtedly show himself such when we begin our course of medicine."

"I believe he will," she responded with a loving smile into Herbert's face and laying a hand tenderly upon his. "I hope to see you both eminent in your chosen profession and doing good to the bodies and souls of your fellow-men. I think there are few more useful men in the world than our cousin Arthur

Conly, and few who are more loved and respected than he; we all love him and have great confidence in his skill."

"I have respected and loved him ever since I can remember," remarked Herbert feelingly, "and can never cease to feel grateful to him as God's instrument in the saving of my mother's life."

"Yes," she said, "I can never forget his kindness at that critical time in my life, and I believe we have all loved him even better since that than before."

"I think you are right about that, mother; I know you are so far as I am concerned," Harold said, tears starting to his eyes. "Ah, when we heard of the danger and suffering you had passed through, we both felt that life without our mother would scarcely be a blessing."

Just then Rosie and Walter came in looking bright and happy.

"Ah, mamma, it is so delightful to have you at home again!" exclaimed the former.

"We missed you sadly, kind as everybody was to us," added Walter, putting his arm round her neck and gazing with ardent affection into her eyes, then kissing her on cheek and lips.

"I suppose it was a little hard for my baby boy to do without his mother," she returned laughingly, holding him in a close embrace.

"Ah, mamma, I can take that name from you easily enough, because I know it is only your pet name for your youngest son, but I'd be vexed enough if anybody else should call me a baby."

"You might well laugh at the absurdity if any one should, Walter," Harold remarked, regarding his little brother with an affectionate look and smile, "for you are really a manly young fellow. I expect to be very proud of you one of these days."

"And I am that already," said Herbert, "for the captain tells me you are a fine scholar for a lad of your years. Besides, I know you are a good and dutiful son to mamma."

"Indeed he is that, as all my boys are," the mother said, regarding the three with loving looks.

"And can you not say as much for your daughters too, mamma—at least for Elsie and Vi?" asked Rosie in playful tone, but with a wistful look.

"I can indeed, for them and for Rosie also," the mother answered, smiling affectionately upon her. "My daughters are all great blessings for which I thank my heavenly Father every day of my life. But now let us have our morning chapter together," opening her Bible as she spoke.

The morning was bright and fair, and it was a cheerful, bright-faced party that presently surrounded the breakfast-table.

"Saturday morning, so only two hours for lessons to-day," remarked Walter in a tone of satisfaction, breaking a slight pause in the conversation.

"What! my scholarly little grandson rejoicing in release from the pursuit of knowledge?" exclaimed Mr. Dinsmore in mock surprise and disapproval.

"Ah, grandpa, you are just in sport, I know," laughed Walter. "But don't you believe these older fellows, Mr. Croly and my two brothers, are glad of their holiday? I just know they are."

"Judging others by yourself, after the manner of older people, eh?"

"Yes, sir; and I'd like to know what's going to be done to-day."

"Well, I believe I can inform you. Everybody who wants to go, and has been faithful in attendance to preliminary duties, will spend the day, by invitation, at the Oaks; Rosie's day and yours beginning when your two hours of school duties are over."

"Oh, I like that! I'm glad, Cousin Mary, that you are to see the place, it is so lovely there, and was mamma's home when she was a little girl and when she grew to be a young lady; and there are the rooms that used to be hers, and the one she was married in."

"I shall be greatly interested in looking at them all, as well as glad to visit Cousin Horace and his family," returned Miss Keith.

"I believe we are all invited?" Edward remarked interrogatively, turning to his wife.

"Yes, my dear," Zoe replied, "even to the babies, who, I hope, will have a good time together in the nursery or out in the grounds."

"Yes," said Rosie, "Sisters Elsie and Violet were talking of going with all the children and young folks of each family. Aunt Rosie too expects to be there with her husband and all the children. The Howards are going also, the Conlys too; so that we shall be the same large party that were here yesterday."

"And next week," said Zoe, "we are all to assemble at Woodburn one day, at the Laurels on another, then at Fairview, and afterward at Roseland."

"What a grand time we shall have!" continued Rosie; "and how can anybody be expected to give his or her mind to lessons? I have serious thoughts of petitioning my big brother—the captain—for a week of holidays."

"How would it do to beg off from attendance upon the parties in order to do justice to your studies?" asked her grandfather in the tone of one suggesting an agreeable alternative.

"O grandpa, I couldn't think of being so very impolite," she exclaimed. "Surely you must know that my absence would spoil all the fun and seriously interfere with any enjoyment others might find in being there if I were with them!"

"But then we ought, any of us, to be willing to forego our own enjoyment for the sake of your improvement in your beloved studies, Rosie dear," said Herbert in tones of brotherly affection.

"Ah, but I could not think of allowing such self-denial for my sake!" she exclaimed. "I should even prefer rising an hour earlier in the morning, or toiling over my tasks an hour later at night; and that is what I think I shall do, if the captain proves obdurate in regard to the granting of the holidays."

"Which he will if I'm not greatly mistaken," said Walter. "He said we were to go on with our studies till the time for our usual summer trip up North, and he's a man to stick to his word if there ever was one."

"Quite a strong recommendation, Walter," laughed Mrs. Dinsmore, "and I really think the captain is deserving of it."

"The captain is a very agreeable man to have

a chat with," remarked Croly. "I have seldom been more interested than I was yesterday in a little talk I had with him in regard to mining interests in the far West."

"Yes; he owns property out there in which there are mines of great value," said Harold.

"Ah? I was not aware of that fact, and he did not mention it," returned Croly; "but in reply to a remark of mine, that I had been paying some attention to mineralogy and thought of going out to examine some land father owns in Arizona, he gave me a good deal of interesting information, such as I have not been able to find in any publication on the subject that I have got hold of as yet."

"And should you question him on naval matters, or the history of our wars—or indeed history of any part of the world, I believe he could furnish all the information you might happen to want," said Herbert.

"Yes," said Walter, "it's my decided belief that Brother Levis knows about as much on almost every subject as you could find in any of the cyclopædias."

"That's very strong, Walter," laughed Edward. "The captain is, without doubt, a highly educated, intelligent, and well-read man, yet hardly a walking cyclopædia; a compliment at which no one would laugh more heartily than himself, for he hasn't a particle of self-conceit in his make-up."

"Now you are complimenting him very highly, Ned," said Mr. Dinsmore, "yet are not saying more than he deserves. I know of no man for whom I have a higher esteem than Captain Raymond."

"And I can echo my father's sentiments. He is a noble Christian man, the best of husbands and fathers," said Mrs. Travilla. "I know of no man with whom I could feel better satisfied as the husband of one of my daughters. Evidently he makes Violet very happy."

"And his children from the oldest to the youngest fairly idolize him," remarked Zoe.

"And you do not object to him as a brother-in-law?" said Rosie interrogatively.

"On the contrary I like him extremely in that capacity," was the quick, emphatic rejoinder.

"Mamma," said Rosie insinuatingly, "Captain Raymond thinks a great deal of you, and as you are his mother, he ought to do as you say; most assuredly in regard to his treatment of your own children. Won't you please send him word this morning that we ought to be allowed a holiday next week? Do now; there's a good, kind mamma."

"Would you have me say what I do not

think, Rosie dear?" queried her mother in return, and with an amused look into the bright eyes of her youngest daughter.

"Ah, mamma, how can you be so severe?" exclaimed Rosie. "Just think how trying to Walter and me to have to set off for lessons at Woodburn not only to-day, but every day next week, when you have only been with us for a day now since your return from your trip to the North."

"For that very reason you and I ought to go willingly and without any fuss," interposed Walter, with manly decision of air and tone. "Besides, as I said before, I know it would be perfectly useless to try to get Brother Levis to change his mind about the matter."

"Then, my wise younger brother, I'll not petition for your release from to-day's tasks, or those of next week," said Rosie.

"Oh, has anything been seen of last night's burglar?" asked Croly, breaking the slight pause following upon Rosie's last remark.

"I have heard nothing of him," replied Edward, "and indeed had forgotten his existence until you spoke, Mr. Croly."

"And poor Polly. Has she been seen?" inquired Mary Keith.

The answer was in the negative; no one had seen or heard of her.

"Ah well, then I suppose she must have found her way back to Woodburn," said Mary.

"By the way, Cousin Mary, how would you like to drive over there this morning?" asked Edward. "They will hardly expect us at the Oaks before eleven o'clock, and Woodburn lies but little out of our way in going."

"But," returned Miss Keith, "we might perhaps hinder Cousin Vi in her preparations for the day's outing."

"I am going to drive you over and call for Vi and the little ones on the way," said Grandma Elsie. "I think we shall find her ready to go on with us after we have had a little call, just for you to see the place. Then the captain will come somewhat later with his children and mine."

"And how is Cousin Ronald to get there, mamma?" asked Walter.

"Probably in the captain's carriage, or on one of his horses," she replied; "the dear old gentleman can go when and how he likes. All such questions were not settled last night, but I know there will be no difficulty in his way, or that of any other invited guest, in getting there comfortably and in good season."

"I'm glad of that, mamma," returned Walter; "I'm very fond of Cousin Ronald and wouldn't have him stay away for anything."

At that remark several furtive, smiling glances were exchanged by the brothers and sisters about the table.

"He is a very pleasant old gentleman," said Mrs. Dinsmore, "and I haven't a doubt will add a great deal to the enjoyment of the company."

"Yes, madam," said Croly. "I saw comparatively little of him yesterday, but quite enough to make me desire a further acquaintance."

"Oh, by the way Will, shall we walk, ride, or drive over to the Oaks to-day?" asked Harold.

"I am ready for any way that suits you, sir," replied Croly.

"Well," said Mr. Dinsmore, "I see every one is ready to leave the table. We will have prayers at once, and afterward settle all such questions in regard to the doings of the day."

## CHAPTER X.

"Mamma," said Rosie, following her mother out to the veranda when prayers were over, "if you approve I will go up at once and dress for the day, getting Walter to do the same. It won't take us long; then I'd like to drive over immediately to Woodburn and coax Brother Levis to let us all begin lessons at once, that we may get through and off to the Oaks sooner than we would otherwise."

"Very well, my child, I will order the carriage; for I think it would be the better plan for you to drive over, as the roads are dusty," was the indulgent reply.

"Yes," said Walter, who had followed and was now close behind them, "I like that plan, for walking one would have to take either the very dusty road or the wet grass; and I'd like to get through lessons as early as possible, too. So I'm off to dress," and away he ran, Rosie following. Just then the telephone bell rang, and Rosie hastening to the instrument found that Captain Raymond was calling from Woodburn to say that his pupils there had requested permission to begin school duties half an hour earlier than usual, that so they might be ready the sooner to drive over to the Oaks; that he had given consent, and would grant the same privilege to Rosie and Walter, if such was their desire, and they would come immediately.

"Thank you, sir. We will be there in a few minutes," returned Rosie, then ran away to hurry through her preparations, while her mother took her place at the telephone to send a message to Violet, to the effect that she and their Cousin Mary might be expected at Woodburn about ten o'clock to make a short call, after which they would go on to the Oaks, taking her and her little ones with them if that arrangement suited her convenience.

"Thank you, mother dear," came back in Violet's own sweet tones, "I shall be glad to see both you and Cousin Mary, and you will find me and my babies ready to accept your kind invitation."

Rosie and Walter made haste with their toilets, were presently in the carriage, and reached Woodburn just in season to take part in the opening school exercises.

All went prosperously that morning; the lessons had been thoroughly prepared, the recitations were so good that the captain felt entitled to bestow unstinted praise, and his pupils were dismissed from the school-room in gayest spirits.

"How very quiet the house seems!" exclaimed Lulu as they passed into the hall.

"Yes," said her father; "Cousin Ronald, your mamma, and the little ones have gone on to the Oaks, and now we will follow them as soon as you are all ready. Our large family carriage is in waiting; it will hold us all nicely."

They had only to put on their hats and gather up a few little things they wanted to take with them, and they drove away, a merry, laughing, jovial little party, so full of fun and frolic that time passed very quickly, and all were surprised when they found the carriage turning in at the great gates opening upon the beautiful grounds of the place that had been Elsie's home in her girlhood's days.

The chat and laughter suddenly ceased, and all eyes turned upon the lovely scenes through which they were passing. They were not entirely new to any of them, and only comparatively so to Marian, as she had already been there several times.

They were almost the last to arrive of all the large company of invited guests, and as they neared the mansion there could be seen, here and there on the lawn and in the shaded alleys, groups of grown people and of children, some sitting in the shade of the trees, others sauntering about or playing merry, romping games, while filling the air with their shouts and gleeful laughter.

A cordial welcome was given the captain and his pupils, who quickly made themselves at home in the grounds, scattering here and there among other guests, according to inclination or convenience.

The captain, having exchanged greetings with his host, hostess, and other friends and relatives, glanced about in search of his wife.

"You are looking for Vi, captain?" Grandma Elsie said inquiringly and with a smile. "She is engaged in piloting Cousin Mary about, showing her the places made memorable by having been the scenes of notable events in her mother's life when this was her own and her father's home. I believe they have gone down to what is still called Elsie's arbor."

"Ah?" he returned, "and my companionship would hardly be welcome just at present, I presume."

"I cannot say, sir, but see no reason why it should not be," she answered, and thanking her, he at once set off in the direction of the arbor, which was of course no unknown spot to him.

He found the ladies there, sitting together, gazing out upon the lovely landscape—the verdant valley, the clear waters of the swiftly flowing river, and the woods clad in the deep green of their summer robes. Violet was speaking in low, feeling tones, Mary listening evidently with intense interest. Violet had been telling of scenes and occurrences described in "Elsie's girlhood"—the time when Arthur, in a fury of passion because she refused to advance him money without her father's knowledge and consent, even went so far as to strike her, and was immediately soundly thrashed for it by Mr. Travilla; the time when Jackson, her discarded lover, discarded at first in obedience to her father's command, afterward loathed by her when she had learned for herself that he was a villain of deepest dye instead of the honorable, virtuous man she had formerly esteemed him, came so unexpectedly upon her there, sitting alone and undefended, and with a loaded pistol threatened her life unless she would promise never to marry Mr. Travilla; but now Violet's theme was her father's confession of his love, and her mother's glad surprise—the sweet story told to her by that mother herself since the dear father's death.

"Mamma told it to me after I had heard the same sweet story from the lips of my own dear husband," were the words that reached the captain's ear as he stepped into the arbor, and as she turned at the sound their eyes met with a look of love as ardent and intense as any ever bestowed by either one upon the other: they were as truly lovers now as they had been five years before.

"Excuse me, ladies," he said with a bow and smile, "I do not wish to intrude, and will go away at once if my company is not desired."

"It is no intrusion, I am sure," was the reply of Miss Keith, while Violet said with a look of pleasure: "We are only too glad to have you with us, my dear. You have come in the nick of time, for I have just finished my story, which, though new to cousin, would have been old to you."

She made room for him by her side as she spoke. He took the offered seat, and they talked for a little of the lovely grounds and the beauty of the view from that point; then rose and walked back to the house, conversing as they went.

Violet led the way to the grassy lawn upon which opened the glass doors of what had been in former years her mother's sitting-room, and through them into the room itself.

"This and the dressing and bed rooms beyond were mamma's apartments while living here,"

she said, "and loving his eldest sister as he
does, Uncle Horace has kept them furnished
all these years almost precisely as they were
when she occupied them."

"I should think he would," said Mary Keith,
sending keenly interested and admiring glances
from side to side; "it is all so lovely that I
should not want to change a single thing, even
if I did not care to keep them just so in remem-
brance of her, as I certainly should."

Mr. Horace Dinsmore, Jr., came in at that
instant.

"Ah, Vi," he said, "so you are showing your
mother's old rooms to Cousin Mary. That is
right. I spent many a happy hour here with
that dear sister when I was but a little fellow,
for, as I presume you know, she is twelve years
older than I.

"Ah, how well I remember the heartache it
gave me when I was told of her approaching
marriage, and that she would then leave our
home for Mr. Travilla's at Ion. I could scarce
forgive him for robbing me of my sister. In
fact I refused my consent, but to my surprise
and chagrin found that it made no difference."

He led the way into the dressing-room.
"This," he said, "is where I found her standing in her beautiful bridal robes, as the hour
drew near when she was to be given to Travilla.

Oh, how beautiful she was! I can see her yet —the lovely, blushing, smiling face, the shining hair adorned with orange-blossoms, and the slender, graceful figure half concealed by the folds of rich white satin and a cloud of mist-like lace. I remember exclaiming, 'You look like an angel, only without the wings!' and how I wanted to hug her, but had been forbidden lest I should spoil or disarrange some of her finery; and what a heartache I had at the thought that she was never to be the same to me again—so entirely our own—as she had been before. She called me to come and kiss her, and oh, what a strong effort it cost to refrain from giving the forbidden hug! but she promised me an opportunity to give it before she went; and the promise was remembered and kept."

"Did you not hug papa instead, Uncle Horace?" queried Violet between a smile and a tear, for she was thinking of that dear parent as gone from among them never to return.

"Yes," he said, "he kindly invited me to use him as a substitute for my sister, which I did heartily, for he was a great favorite with me, in spite of his robbing me of her."

"In which room of the house was Cousin Elsie married?" asked Mary.

"Come and I will show you, pointing out the

precise spot where she stood during the ceremony," replied Mr. Dinsmore, leading the way,
the others willingly following.

He redeemed his promise, gave a description
of the adornment of the rooms on that memorable occasion, of the grounds also, and ended
with the bride's farewell to relatives and near
and dear friends, especially her almost idolized
father.

"Yes," said Violet, "mamma has always
loved grandpa so very, very dearly, and his love
for her is, I believe, quite as great.   Ah, uncle,
let us take cousin to the hall and show her the
niche from which mamma once fell when quite
a little girl."

"And I a baby boy," he returned with a
smile as he led the way; "but it was not from
a niche she fell, Vi, but from a chair on the
edge of which she stood, trying to reach up to
hide a toy mouse behind the statue there.   The
chair slipped from under her; to save herself
from falling she caught wildly at the legs of
the statue, and she and it came down together
with a crash upon the marble floor.   There is
the niche," pointing it out, for they had
reached the hall while he spoke; "the figure
occupying it now is one purchased to replace
that broken by its fall with sister at that time."

"Did it fall on her? and was she badly hurt?"

asked Miss Keith, shuddering slightly as she spoke.

"No," replied Mr. Dinsmore, "not quite upon her, but so nearly that she had a very narrow escape from being crushed by it; she was stunned and bruised, but that was all, and she was able to join in the sports of the next day." *

"Mary, that was in the winter which your aunts Mildred and Annis spent here," remarked Violet. "I suppose you have heard something of that?"

"Yes, I think I have," said Miss Keith. "Cousin Percy and you, Cousin Horace, were babes at that time, were you not? I think you said a moment since."

"I have been told that we were," Mr. Dinsmore replied with a smile. "Now I think I have shown you about all the places in the house that are interesting from being connected with events in my sister's life. Most of our friends are at present on the verandas or the lawn; shall we go out and join them?"

A prompt assent was given and he led the way. All the invited guests seemed to have arrived; even Dr. Conly, who had been somewhat delayed by professional duties, was there surrounded by the young people, who were all

* See "Mildred's Married Life."

10

fond of him as both relative and physician.
Calhoun, the Dinsmore girls, Evelyn Leland,
Marian McAlpine, Lulu Raymond, Harold and
Herbert Travilla formed another group; but
Calhoun, on seeing Mary Keith approaching,
left the others, advanced to meet her, and after
exchanging with her a pleasant "Good-morning," invited her to a stroll through the
grounds, adding, "I presume you have hardly
seen every part of them yet?"

"No," she replied, as they sauntered on together, and went on to tell to what parts Violet
had taken her.

"Ah," he said, "I am glad the pleasure of
showing the rest was left for me. It is a fine
old place, and being a near relative of the
owners I have seen much of it."

"Yes, and I have been told that Roselands
also is a fine old place," she returned; "and
was not it Cousin Elsie's home at one time?"

"Yes; for several years before her father
bought this place and fitted it up for a home
for himself and her."

"I think it was there she was so very ill
while still quite a little girl?"

"Yes; that was before my time, but when
you visit us there, as I hope to have the pleasure of seeing you do next week, I will show
you the room she occupied; no—I am forget-

ting that the house standing there then was afterward burned down; but it was rebuilt, that part of it being an exact reproduction of those rooms in the old house."

"Burned down, did you say? How did that happen?"

"It was during the war," he replied. "As I remember Roselands on my first sight of it, it was a most desolate place—only the ruins of a house there, the ground ploughed up by cannon, the grand old trees all cut down, the lawn changed to a muddy field, the gardens a desert, neither fences, hedgerows, nor shrubbery left, the fields overgrown with weeds—all the result of that dreadful civil war for which I now see there was no cause but the curse of slavery.

"But," he continued, his voice taking on a more cheerful tone, "many years have passed since then; our dear Cousin Elsie furnished the necessary means for repairing damages so far as money could do it, the passing years have helped, and Roselands again deserves its name; in the eyes of its owners at least it is again a beautiful place, the fields are fertile and scarce anything is left that reminds us of its former desolation."

"I am very glad indeed to hear that," returned Mary, "and shall greatly enjoy seeing it in its renewed beauty. This place it would seem escaped better than Roselands?"

"Far better; indeed had, I believe, suffered only from some years of neglect. It was quite habitable; so uncle kindly gave us all shelter here for a time—that is, until Roselands was ready to receive us."

"That was very kind," responded Mary.

"It was indeed," said Calhoun. "I cannot tell you how strongly I am attached to uncle, Aunt Rose, Cousin Elsie, and indeed the whole family."

Just then a turn in the walk brought them face to face with another small party of young people—the Dinsmore girls, Rosie Travilla, Croly, Harold, and Herbert.

"So here you are!" exclaimed Harold. "We were looking for you and want to take you back near the house. We are to have a small lunch of cake and lemonade handed about to us on the lawn, Aunt Sue says; after that some games to make the time pass pleasantly until the dinner-hour."

"With such inducements held out would it not be well to go with them, Miss Keith?" queried Calhoun.

"Perhaps so," she returned laughingly; "since I heard the lemonade mentioned I have discovered that I am somewhat thirsty."

"And I own that the announcement has had the same effect upon me," he said.

"Then come," said Herbert, leading the way by turning into another shaded alley; "we will reach our destination sooner by this path."

The day passed most pleasantly to all, the greater part of it spent in sports in the open air; a grand dinner, served in the large dining-room of the mansion, taking up an hour or more; then a time of rest and quiet talk underneath the trees or on the verandas; after that more games, followed by a light tea handed the guests where they were, and soon after a pleasant ride or drive homeward.

# CHAPTER XI.

THE next day was Sunday, always religiously kept by every family in the connection. They all met at church in the morning, and most of the Ion and Woodburn people again in the afternoon; first at the school-house on the captain's estate, where an hour was spent in the instruction of the poor whites of the neighborhood, then in the Ion school-house appropriated to the same use for the colored race of the vicinity.

Mary Keith, Harold, Herbert, and their old friend Croly attended and took part in the exercises of both schools; for they were all earnest, active Christian workers, full of zeal for the Master's cause and anxious to win souls for him.

Harold and Herbert dearly loved to talk over with their mother their plans for future usefulness and the necessary preparation for it, and, to their supreme content, contrived to get her to themselves for a time on their return from the scene of that afternoon's labors. The call to tea broke up their conference.

The evening was spent in Bible study, religious conversation, and sacred song.

It had been a day of rest from earthly cares and pleasures, and all rose on Monday morning refreshed and strengthened in mind and body.

That day was spent at the Laurels, very much as Saturday had been at the Oaks; Tuesday at Fairview. Violet claimed her right to be the next entertainer of the connection, so all were invited to spend that day at Woodburn, where preparations for their entertainment had been going on for several days.

Eager, impetuous Lulu was almost wild with delight. "O papa," she said, when she and Grace had exchanged with him their usual affectionate good-morning, "I do just hope we'll give the folks the grandest good time they've had anywhere yet. It's a splendid day, and our grounds never looked more beautiful. I could hardly get dressed for gazing at them through my bedroom windows, and I thanked the Lord over and over again for giving me such a lovely home and dear, kind father," putting her arms round his neck and giving him a second ardent kiss.

"Yes, daughter," he returned, holding her close, "the goodness of our heavenly Father to us is far, far beyond our deserts. I thank him every day for the ability he has given me to make such a delightful home for my wife and children."

"Yes, papa," said Grace, leaning up affectionately against him on his other side, and slipping a hand into his, "I often think how very, very good God has been to us children in giving us such a good, kind father, when so many poor children have cross, drunken fathers who beat and abuse them for just nothing at all, and don't care whether they are comfortably fed and clothed or not."

"It is a sad truth that there are such fathers in the world," he replied, "and some who with all their efforts cannot comfortably feed and clothe their little ones."

"And other poor little ones who have no father or mother," added Grace. "Oh, I do hope God will let me keep my dear father as long as I live."

"Do not allow yourself to be anxious and troubled about that, daughter," the captain responded tenderly, "our heavenly Father knows and will do for each one of us just what is best."

"Papa," said Lulu coaxingly, "don't you think you could excuse us from lessons to-day? There will be so much going on that I know I shall find it very difficult to give my mind to lessons, and I'm sure it will be just the same with the others."

"If I thought it for your good, daughter," he said in reply, "I should certainly say yes; but I do not. If you are diligent you can be ready to receive your young guests by eleven o'clock."

"But I think it will be almost impossible to give my mind to tasks when it is so full of all that's to be done and enjoyed through the day," she sighed.

"I am sure you can if you will exercise sufficient determination," he replied; "you have a strong will, and can put it to good use in forcing Lucilla Raymond to resolutely put aside distracting thoughts and give her mind for a time wholly to her appointed tasks. Show her that if she wants to do right and please her heavenly Father, she will do it for that reason; and if she loves her earthly one as dearly as she says, she will do it to gain his approbation and make his heart glad that he has so good and dutiful an eldest daughter."

"So I will, papa," she said, giving him another affectionate hug, "for oh, I do want to make you glad that I am your very own child, your very, very own, and don't belong to anybody else in the whole world."

"And that I am, papa," Grace said, lifting to his eyes full of ardent filial love. "I am every bit as glad to belong to you as Lu is."

"And I quite as glad to own you, my own

darling little girl," he responded, drawing them both closer into his embrace.

The breakfast-bell rang, and taking a hand of each, he led them down to the lower hall, where they met Violet coming in from the veranda where she and her two little ones had been taking the air.

Pleasant greetings were exchanged with them and with Mr. Lilburn and Marian, who presently joined the family in the breakfast-room. Then all seated themselves, the blessing was asked, and the meal began.

"Cousin Ronald," said Violet, "I hope you will help to entertain our guests to-day by the exercise of your ventriloquial powers, which have not yet been discovered by either Cousin Mary Keith or Mr. Croly."

"I should like to oblige you, cousin," replied the old gentleman, "but I fear I cannot think of anything new in that line."

"Well," she said, "we will hope some bright thoughts may occur to you."

"Perhaps you might borrow a bugle again, sir," remarked Lulu with a little laugh. "I don't believe they've found out yet who that bugler was who played near the lakelet at Ion, when they were in the boat on it."

"No," said Marian, "from something that was said yesterday, I am sure they have not."

"Such being the case, perhaps the fellow may take it into his head to visit the wood here this afternoon or evening," Mr. Lilburn remarked in a quiet tone.

"Oh, I hope he will!" exclaimed Lulu, "and that he'll play longer than he did at Ion. I wonder if he couldn't sing us a song too," she added, smiling archly into Mr. Lilburn's eyes.

"Now perhaps he may if I tell him that a daughter of our entertainers makes the request," returned Mr. Lilburn gravely. "I'll try my influence with him, my dear."

"Oh, thank you, sir!" she exclaimed with a merry laugh. "I am quite sure he will not be able to resist that."

"I just wish we had Maxie here," said Grace, "for then we might have one sing and the other play at the same time."

"That would be fine," laughed her father, "but unfortunately we cannot have Max."

"Oh!" exclaimed Marian with a look of surprise and pleasure, "now I know who was the ventriloquist at Minersville!"

"There now!" cried Grace with a look of dismay, "I ought to be ashamed. I never meant to tell that secret."

"Don't look so troubled, daughter," said the captain, smiling kindly upon her, "there is no great harm done. Marian would probably have found it out before long without any help from you."

"And I'll try to make no bad use of my discovery," added Marian.

"You and papa are very kind," returned Grace, with a slight sigh of relief.

"I suppose this is to be a holiday for the children, captain?" remarked Violet with an inquiring look at her husband.

"Quite a mistake, my dear," he returned pleasantly. "I do not think it good for my pupils to have too many holidays, and have no doubt they will enjoy play all the more for having done a little work first."

"Yes, sir, no doubt we shall," said Marian cheerfully, "and I for one should be very loath to miss the lessons. I enjoy them, and am very grateful to you for taking the trouble to teach me."

"You are as welcome as possible," he returned in the kindest of tones. "Your companionship in her studies is of advantage to my daughter Lulu, and makes very little more work for me."

"You are very kind indeed to look at it in that light, sir," was Marian's response, while Lulu gave him a most grateful, loving look.

Then a voice that seemed to come from the doorway into the hall said: "You are the very best of fathers, sir, always ready to take any amount of trouble for the benefit of any of your children."

"Maxie! where is you? Tum and det some breakfus," exclaimed baby Ned, as he and all the others turned their heads in the direction of the sounds.

But no one was to be seen there.

"Where is Maxie?" queried Ned, almost ready to cry. "Papa tell Maxie tum eat his breakfus."

"Maxie isn't there, son," said the captain pleasantly. "It was Cousin Ronald talking in Maxie's voice."

"Papa," said little Elsie, "maybe Maxie is there, hiding behind the door."

"Do you think so?" returned her father with a smile. "Well, you may go and look, if you wish, and if you find him tell him papa says for him to come immediately to his breakfast."

At that Elsie made haste to get down from her chair, and ran to the door calling, "Maxie, Maxie, papa says, come right to your breakfus dis minute."

Not finding Max at the door, she ran on down the hall, out upon the veranda, looking searchingly from side to side, back again and through the different rooms, calling, "Max, Max, where are you? Papa says, come to your breakfus."

Then on into the breakfast-room she came again, saying with a bewildered look, " Papa, I can't find Max. Where did he go?"

"Don't you remember that papa told you he was not there, daughter?" returned the captain pleasantly. "It was Cousin Ronald who spoke, making his voice sound like Max's."

"Oh, I wish it was Maxie, 'cause I love him and want to see him," returned the baby girl, tears springing to her eyes.

"Never mind, papa's dear little girl," the captain said, lifting her into her chair again; "we may hope to see dear brother Max here one of these days; and then how glad we shall all be!"

"Oh, yes, papa; please write Maxie a letter and tell him Elsie wants him to come soon," she said, smiling through her tears.

The moment family worship was over, Marian, Lulu, and Grace hastened to the school-room, where they were joined a few minutes later by Evelyn Leland, Rosie and Walter Travilla. The lessons had all been thoroughly prepared, so that recitations proceeded rapidly, and by eleven o'clock all were dismissed with permission to spend the remainder of the day in such sports as suited their inclination.

The guests had already begun to arrive, and directly the most of them were scattered through the beautiful grounds exploring every nook and corner of them. Then games were played—lawn tennis, croquet, and others suited to different ages and tastes. A grand dinner followed in due season, after which they sat on the verandas or under the trees or wandered slowly through the wood and the shaded alleys.

Tea was over, the sun near his setting, and somewhat weary with their sports almost all were seated in or near the verandas, when the sound of a bugle broke the stillness, coming apparently from the wood where a number of the young people had been straying only a half-hour before.

"There he is again!" cried Croly, starting to his feet. "Harold, suppose we hurry out yonder and see if we can catch sight of the fellow."

"Oh, not yet," said Grandma Elsie; "let us enjoy his music for a little first. Hark! he is beginning the Star-spangled Banner."

"Very well done," commented Mr. Dinsmore as the last notes died away on the air. Croly looked at Harold and half rose from his chair; but the bugler began again. This time it was a Scottish air, and Marian absently, and scarcely above her breath, sang the words:

> "'Scots wha' hae wi Wallace bled,
> Scots whom Bruce hath often led,
> Welcome to your gory bed,
>     Or to victory.'"

The notes of the bugle died away, and all was quiet for a moment; then Walter broke the silence:

"So that's a Scotch tune, is it, Marian? I heard you singing Scotch words to it—about Wallace and Bruce—and there's scarcely any story I feel more interest in—unless maybe tales of our own Revolution. They were brave fellows, and I like to think I come of the same stock on mamma's side at least."

"Yes, it's a good stock to come of," she answered, her eyes kindling; "none better in my esteem; they have always been a liberty-loving, God-fearing race—the great mass o' them at least. But hark! there's the bugler at it again; nearer, and playing quite another tune."

It was a simple little air, played as a prelude, and presently the bugle ceased, and a man's voice sang:

"Thimble scolding, wife lay dead,
        Heigh-ho, says Thimble.
    My dearest dear, as Defunctum said,
    Death has cabbaged her, oh she's fled,
    With your rolly-pooly, gammon and spinnage,
        Heigh-ho, says Thimble.

"Thimble buried his wife last night,
        Heigh-ho, says Thimble,
    It grieves me to bury my heart's delight
    With a diamond ring on her finger so tight,

With your rolly-pooly, gammon and spinnage,
  Heigh-ho, says Thimble.

"To cut off her finger and get this ring,
  Next came the sexton;
She rose on an end and she gave him a fling;
'You dirty dog, you'll do no such a thing,
  With your rolly-pooly, gammon and spinnage,'
    Off ran the sexton.

"She stalked to her home and she made a great din,
  Heigh-ho, says Thimble;
He poked out his head and he said with a grin,
'You're dead, my dear duck, and I can't let you in,
  With your rolly-pooly, gammon and spinnage,'
    Heigh-ho, says Thimble."

All had listened intently, and for a moment after the song ceased, no one moved or spoke. Then Croly started up, saying: "I'm bound to see that fellow. Come, Harold and Herbert, will you go with me, or must I search for him alone?"

"Oh, I have no objection to going with you," returned Harold with a slight laugh. "I hardly think he can be dangerous, and if he is I must try to defend you, Will."

"And in that case you may stand in need of my services also," said Herbert, joining them as they hurried down the veranda steps and along the drive in the direction from which the sounds of the bugle and the voice had come.

11

"What you doing? what you 'bout?" came just at that instant in a loud, harsh scream, apparently from the same tree-top. "Breakfast-time. Polly wants a cracker. Polly wants a cup of coffee."

The three young men stepped close to the tree and gazed upward among its branches.

"The parrot again!" exclaimed Croly. "Do you see her, boys?"

"Not I," replied Herbert, "but it is quite dark up there where the branches and leaves are so thick."

"So it is," said Croly. "Hi there, Polly! show yourself."

"Go 'way!" screamed the harsh voice.

"Come down, Polly; we won't hurt you," said Harold.

"Polly's hungry; Polly wants a cracker," responded the harsh voice.

"Come down, and if you are the good bird you seem, you shall have a cracker and a cup of coffee," he promised; but the only reply was a sound as of the fluttering and flapping of wings that seemed to leave the tree and go farther away till lost in the distance.

"Gone!" said Croly; "and I did not catch so much as a glimpse of her. Did anybody else?"

"And you haven't found the bugler either," remarked Mary Keith.

"No," laughed Calhoun Conly, sitting beside her, "they are not very successful hunters."

"Do you think you could do better, Cal?" asked Herbert, as he and his two companions came leisurely up the steps into the veranda.

"Well, I hardly think I should do worse," returned Calhoun lightly.

"Then suppose you start out on the quest, find that bugler, and coax him to give us another tune."

Some soft, low notes came to their ears at that moment, as if in reply; they seemed to issue from the depths of the wood, and the listeners almost held their breath to catch them. As they died away Croly spoke again.

"He seems to have made quite a circuit to escape us; and why on earth should he? for he surely has no reason to fear we would do him harm."

"Bashful, perhaps," suggested Edward. "But why care to see him? Is not hearing enough?"

"If Mr. Croly were a woman, I would suggest that he was probably actuated by curiosity," laughed Mary Keith; "but since he belongs to the other sex, it must be supposed to be something else."

"Dear me, Miss Keith, who would ever have dreamed you could be so severe? You who belong to the gentler sex?" returned Croly, in a feignedly mortified tone.

"Hark! there he is at it again!" exclaimed Maud Dinsmore, as distant bugle notes once more came softly to the ear. "If you want to catch him, I advise you to hasten in the direction of those sounds, Mr. Croly."

"Hardly worth while, since he is so adroit at getting out of the way," sighed Croly, sinking into a chair as if quite exhausted with the efforts already made.

"Never say die, Mr. Croly," laughed Rosie Travilla. "Gather up your strength and pursue the investigation. 'Try, try, try again,' is an excellent motto."

"Yes, Miss Rosie, in some cases, but perhaps not in this, where the game seems to be hardly worth the candle."

"Oh!" exclaimed Walter, "the music seems to be coming nearer! Hadn't you fellows better start out and try again to catch the player? You might be more successful this time. I wouldn't like to give it up so if I were in your place."

"Then suppose you put yourself in our place, and start out in quest of him," suggested his brother Harold.

"I've no objections; I'm not afraid of him," returned Walter, jumping up; "but if you'd

like to go with me, Cousin Ronald?" turning toward the old gentleman, as if with a
sudden thought, "I'd be very glad to have
you."

Mr. Lilburn rose as if to comply with the request, but Mrs. Travilla interposed.

"Oh, no, my son," she said; "Cousin Ronald
must feel tired after all the exertion he has
made to-day."

"And I offer myself as a substitute," said Dr.
Conly, rising. "If the fellow should happen
to be vicious enough to knock you down, Walter, it might be well to have the doctor along
to see to your hurts."

"Pshaw! I'm not a bit afraid of him," said
Walter.

"But your lack of fear is no positive proof
that he is entirely harmless; so I think it
would be as well for you to have an elder
brother along," remarked Herbert, following
them down the veranda steps.

"Oh, come along then, and if the fellow
attacks us, I'll do my best to defend you,"
laughed Walter; and the three set off together
for the wood.

"Is this the bugler's first visit to your place,
captain?" asked Croly.

"I really do not remember having heard his
bugle about here before," was the reply in a

meditative tone, "but I do not imagine him a person likely to do any harm."

"Why, there is the hack from Union turning in at the great gates!" exclaimed Lulu. "We must be going to have a visitor."

It came rapidly up the drive and paused before the entrance; the door was thrown open, and a rather young-looking man alighted, the captain at the same time rising from his chair and stepping forward to greet him.

"Captain Raymond?" the stranger said inquiringly, lifting his hat as he spoke.

At that Mr. Lilburn sprang to his feet and came forward, exclaiming, "What, Hugh, my mon, is it you?" grasping the young man's hand and giving it a hearty shake. "It's one o' my sons, captain," turning glad, shining eyes upon his host. "I was not expecting him, for he had given me no warning of his coming."

"You are very welcome, sir," said the captain, taking the hand of the young man in a cordial grasp.

At that Grandma Elsie, Mr. and Mrs. Dinsmore, and Violet hastened forward with like greetings and expressions of pleasure at seeing him again after the lapse of years since their weeks of friendly intercourse at the sea-shore.

"But you should be my guest, cousin," said Mrs. Travilla. "We shall be going home presently, and will be most happy to have you accompany us."

"Oh, no, mother, it will not do for you to rob us of our guest so promptly," said Captain Raymond.

"No, indeed, mother dear, we must have Cousin Hugh here with his father, at least for the first few days," Violet hastened to say; and so it was settled after a little more discussion, and a servant was dispatched to the village for Hugh's baggage.

Just as that matter was fairly arranged, Dr. Conly, Herbert, and Walter returned to the house.

When they and Hugh had been introduced and had exchanged greetings, Croly inquired if they had succeeded in catching the bugler.

"No, we didn't get so much as a glimpse of him," returned Walter. "But then you see it was growing quite dark in the wood, so that it wasn't so very difficult for a nimble-footed fellow to make his escape."

## CHAPTER XII.

THE Conlys claimed it as their privilege to entertain the connection on the following day, and before leaving Woodburn that evening gave Mr. Hugh Lilburn a cordial invitation to make one of the company, which he accepted with evident pleasure.

Again the weather was delightful, every one in good health and spirits, and the host and hostess were most kind and attentive, making each guest feel welcome and at home.

Roselands was again a beautiful place; its fields in a higher state of cultivation than ever before, yielding excellent crops, Calhoun having proved himself a wise, industrious, scientific planter and manager, while Arthur assisted with his advice and professional gains; so that they had at length succeeded in paying off all indebtedness and could feel that the estate was now really their own.

Calhoun greatly enjoyed showing Mary Keith about the house and grounds; calling her attention particularly to such parts of them as were more especially associated with the experiences of his Cousin Elsie's early life; for Mary was a deeply interested listener to everything he had to tell on the subject.

Toward tea-time all had gathered on the verandas and the lawn in front of the house. The young people and little ones were somewhat weary with romping games and roaming over the grounds, so that very little was going on among them except a bit of quiet chat here and there between some of the older people.

Walter, always eager for the sports Cousin Ronald could make for them with his ventriloquism, stepped to the back of the old gentleman's chair and made a whispered request for an exertion of his skill in that line.

"Wait a bit, laddie, and I'll see what can be done," replied Mr. Lilburn, ever willing to indulge the boy, who was a great favorite with him.

Walter took possession of a vacant chair near at hand, and patiently waited. Mr. Lilburn gave his son a slight sign, hardly noticed by any one else, and almost immediately the notes of a flute came softly to the ear as if from some distance.

Instantly conversation was hushed and all listened intently. It seemed but a prelude, and presently a rich tenor voice struck in and sang

a pretty Scotch ballad, the flute playing an ac-
companiment.

Many looks of surprise were exchanged, for
surely Cousin Ronald could not be responsible
for it all; he could not both sing and play the
flute at the same time, and the questions, "Who
are they? What does it mean?" passed from
one to another.

"What you doing? what you 'bout?"
screamed a harsh voice, apparently from a
tree-top near at hand.

"None o' your business," croaked another.

Walter started up and whispered in the old
gentleman's ear, "Why, Cousin Ronald, are
there two of you to-night? or—no, it can't be
that Max is here?"

"No, no, laddie, that guess is wide of the
mark," laughed Mr. Lilburn in return, while
little Elsie Raymond exclaimed, "Two Pollies!
and we have only one at our house."

"Why, it's very odd," remarked Lulu. "I
really thought my Polly was the only one in
this neighborhood."

"I think the voice of the first one was hers,"
said Mary Keith, "and the same too that we
heard at Ion; I recognized it when I saw and
heard her at Woodburn; but the other voice is a
little different."

"Yes, a little harsher," said Rosie, "like a

male voice. Polly must have hunted up a mate somewhere."

"Two cups of coffee!" screamed the first voice. "Polly wants her breakfast."

"Not breakfast, Polly, but supper," laughed Walter. "You don't seem to know the time o' day."

"Supper! Polly wants her supper," croaked the second voice. "Polly's hungry."

"Just wait a bit," laughed Walter; "we'll all be getting ours presently, and if you are good birds probably you'll get some too."

At that moment a bell rang.

"There's the call to it now," said Calhoun. "Walk in, ladies and gentlemen—children too —and the pollies shall have theirs if they will follow with the crowd."

Every one accepted the invitation, and they were soon seated about the tables; it took several to accommodate them all. A moment's hush, then Cousin Ronald was requested to ask a blessing, and did so in a few words spoken in reverent tones. The guests were then helped, and the meal began, a buzz of subdued conversation accompanying it.

The parrot at Woodburn had learned many words and sentences since her arrival there; during Mr. Lilburn's visit he and she had become well acquainted, and under his tuition her vocabulary had been very considerably increased, so that she could upon occasion, or when so disposed, make herself a very entertaining companion.

Presently her voice, or one very like it, was heard above the clatter of plates, knives and forks, and the buzz of talk, coming seemingly from the mantelpiece some yards in Mr. Lilburn's rear.

"Polly wants her supper. What you 'bout? Polly's hungry."

"Stop your noise, Polly," promptly responded the other parrot's voice.

"Cup o' coffee for Polly, Mamma Vi," promptly demanded the first voice.

"Miss Ella rules here," laughingly returned Violet, "but even she cannot serve you unless you show yourselves."

"Why, where is dem?" queried little Ned, gazing in wide-eyed wonder in the direction from which the sounds had seemed to come. "Me tan't see de pollies."

"Nor can I, Neddie boy," said his Uncle Edward.

But at that instant subdued voices were heard conversing in quiet tones, apparently outside upon the veranda, but close to an open door leading into the dining-room.

"That supper smells mighty good, Bill."

"So it does, Pat. Come now, let's just step in and help ourselves, seein' as they doan't hev perliteness enuff to ask us in or hand out so much as a bite o' victuals to us."

"Let's wait our turn, though, and perhaps we'll get an invite when they're well filled theirselves."

"You're not afeared they'll eat it all theirselves?"

"Huh! no; how could they? There's loads and loads of grub there; plenty for them and us too."

"Yaas, 'bout enuff to feed a regirment."

Conversation about the table had ceased; every one was gazing in the direction from which the sounds of the talk between the two rough men seemed to come.

"Whar dem fellers? I doan see 'em!" exclaimed a colored lad engaged in waiting on the table; "hear deir talkin' plain 'nuff, though."

"Ha, ha!" laughed one of the strange voices, "is that so, darky? Then I reckon your hearing's some better'n your sight."

"Impident rascal!" returned the colored lad wrathfully. "Mr. Cal, I'll go drive 'im out ef you say so, sir."

"Yes, do so at once, Hector," returned Calhoun. "We don't want tramps about to-day, and he seems a decidedly impudent one."

ing our guests, Art.; Uncle Horace's plate wants replenishing; the captain's too."

"Polly's hungry; poor old Polly, poor old soul!" screamed from the mantelpiece again the voice that sounded like that of Lulu's pet. "Breakfast-time. Polly wants coffee."

"Hush, Polly! be quiet, Polly!" croaked the other voice. "Eat your cracker and go to sleep."

"Hold your tongue, Poll," screamed the first. "Polly wants a cup of coffee."

Hector, who was a new servant, stood looking this way and that, gasping and rolling up his eyes in terror, but the others, who were tolerably well acquainted, by hearsay at least, with Mr. Lilburn's ventriloquial powers, had by this time recalled what they had heard on that subject, and went quietly about waiting upon the guests.

Croly and Mary Keith had been most interested listeners, and when an instant's lull occurred, after the parrot-like screams, the former said: "Well, ladies and gentlemen, I am now fully convinced that we have, at least, one ventriloquist among us, though which of you it is I have not been quite able to decide."

"It may, perhaps, be easier to decide who it is not," remarked the elder Mr. Dinsmore, with an amused smile.

12

"Very true, sir," said Croly, "and I have come to the conclusion that it is not yourself, Captain Raymond, Doctor Conly, or my friends Harold or Herbert Travilla." With the last words he looked inquiringly at each of the other gentlemen present. Not one of them seemed to him to look conscious, and he felt that his question still remained unsolved.

Hector, still trembling with fright, and now and then sending a timorous glance in the direction of the door at which the tramps had last been heard, had listened in wondering surprise to the talk about the ventriloquist.

"What dat, Scip?" he asked in shaking undertones, plucking at the sleeve of a fellow servant, "dat vent-vent-erquis? Dis chile neber hear of dat sort of ting afore."

"You jess g'long an' look fer it then," returned Scip loftily. "'Pears like maybe you find him in de parlor yonder behind de doah."

The children had been looking and listening, wondering where the men and the parrots were.

"Papa, where is de mans and birds? de pollies dat talked so loud?" asked little Eric Leland. "Me don't see dem."

"No; they can only be heard, not seen," laughed his father, "while little fellows—like my Eric, you know—should be seen and not heard when at table with so many older people."

"Big folks talk very much, papa," remarked the little one, smiling up into his father's face.

"So they do, and so may you when you grow big," returned his father. "And now, when at home with no strangers by, you may talk too."

"Well, Hector, suppose you take Scip's advice and go and look for those tramps," said Dr. Conly, addressing the frightened, perplexed-looking young servant-man. "Don't be afraid; I promise to cure your hurts if you get any in trying to put them out."

But Hector stood where he was as if rooted to the spot, shaking his head gloomily in response to the doctor's suggestions.

"No, tank you, doctah, sah, but dis chile radder stay cured widout bein' hurted fus," he answered, retreating a little farther from the parlor door as he spoke.

"Then come and make yourself useful," said Ella. "Get your salver and hand this cup of coffee to Mr. Lilburn."

Hector obeyed, and Cousin Ronald, giving him a humorous look as he took his cup from the salver, asked: "Are you really going to leave those tramps in the parlor yonder to carry off whatever they please?"

"Why, sah, dis chile ain't so powerful strong dat he kin fight two big fellers widout nobody to help wid the business," grumbled Hector. looking very black at the suggestion.

"Oh, Hector, don't be such a coward," exclaimed Walter Travilla. "I'm not very big or strong, but, if mamma will let me, I'll go along and protect you from them while you put them out. I may, mayn't I, mamma?" giving her an inquiring look as he rose from his chair.

But at that moment one of the strange voices was again heard at the door opening on the veranda.

"Never mind, little feller; we're out here and going off now; and we haven't taken a pin's worth, for we're honest chaps if we are poor and sometimes ask for a bite o' victuals."

"Yaas, that's so," drawled the other voice.

A sound like that of retreating footsteps followed; then all was quiet, and Hector drew a long breath of relief.

"Glad dey's gone," he said presently, then went briskly about his business.

It was still early, not yet sundown, when those of the guests who had little ones took leave of their kind entertainers, and started for their homes. Edward and Zoe, with their twin babies, were among the first. Herbert, too, excused himself, and on the plea of a letter to write for the next mail went with them, riding his horse beside the carriage in which the others were seated.

They took a short cut through a bit of woods and were moving rather leisurely along, chatting about Cousin Ronald's tricks of the afternoon and speculating upon the seeming fact that he must have a coadjutor, when Herbert suddenly reined in his steed, backing him away from the vehicle, and at the same time calling out in a quick, imperative, excited tone to the driver: "Rein in your horses, Solon! Quick, quick, back them for your life!"

Even while he spoke the order was obeyed, yet barely in time; for at that instant a great tree came down with a heavy crash, falling across the road directly in front of the horses and so close that it grazed their noses as it passed.

Zoe, throwing an arm round her husband's neck and clasping her babies close with the other, gave one terrified shriek, then for several minutes all sat in horror-struck silence, feeling that they had escaped by but a hair's-breadth from sudden, horrible death. Edward's arm was about her waist, and he drew her closer and closer yet, with a gesture of mute tenderness.

"O Ned, dear Ned, how near we've been to death! we and our darlings," she exclaimed, bursting into tears and sobs.

"Yes," he said in trembling tones. "Oh, thank the Lord for his goodness! The Lord first, and then you, Herbert," for his brother was now close by the side of the carriage again.

"No thanks are due me, dear Ned," he replied, with emotion, "but let us thank the Lord that he put it into my heart to come along with you, and directed my eyes to the tree as it swayed slightly, preparatory to its sudden fall. Look, Zoe, what a large, heavy one it is—one of the old monarchs of the wood and still hale and vigorous in appearance. Who would ever have expected it to fall so suddenly and swiftly?"

"I hardly want to," she said, shuddering; "it seems so like a dreadful foe that had tried to kill my husband, my darling babies, and myself."

"How the horses are trembling with fright!" exclaimed Edward. "Poor fellows! it is no wonder, for if I am not mistaken the tree actually grazed their noses as it fell."

"Yes, sah, it did dat berry ting," said Solon, who had alighted and was stroking and patting the terrified steeds, "an' dey mos' tinks dey's half killed. I dunno how we's goin' fer to git 'long hyar, Mr. Ed'ard, sah; cayn't drive ober dis big tree no how 'tall."

"No, but perhaps we can manage to go round it; or better still, we'll turn and drive back till

we can get into the high-road again. But drive
slowly, till your horses recover, in a measure at
least, from their fright."

"Yes, I think that is the best we can do,"
said Herbert, wheeling about and trotting on
ahead.

The shock to Zoe had been very severe. All
the way home she was shuddering, trembling,
sobbing hysterically, and clinging to her husband and babies as though in terror lest they
should be suddenly torn from her arms.

In vain Edward tried to sooth and quiet her,
clasping her close and calling her by every endearing name; telling her the danger was a
thing of the past; that their heavenly Father
had mercifully preserved and shielded them,
and they had every reason to rest with quietness
and assurance in his protecting care.

"Yes, yes, I know it all, dear Ned," she
sobbed, "but have patience with me, dear; my
nerves are all unstrung and I cannot be calm
and quiet; I cannot help trembling, or keep
back the tears, though I am thankful, oh, so
thankful! that not one of us was killed or even
hurt."

"No; it was a wonderful escape," he said in
moved tones; "a wonderful evidence of the
goodness of God to all of us; and thankful I am
that even the horses escaped injury."

# CHAPTER XIII.

Solon had an exciting tale to tell in the kitchen while he gave his horses a brief rest before returning to Roselands for the remaining members of the family.

It was listened to with intense interest, and many ejaculations of astonishment at the sudden fall of the tree and of thankfulness that no one was hurt.

"My!" exclaimed the cook, "it would 'a' been a' awful thing if Miss Elsie been 'long and got killed wid dat tree a-fallin' onto her."

"Yes, tank de good Lord dat she wasn't dar," said Solon; "but I reckon she'd mos' rather be killed her own self dan have such ting happen to Marse Edward an' Miss Zoe and de babies."

"Course," put in another servant; "Miss Elsie she's got de kindest heart in de world, and she loves her chillen and gran'chillen better'n her own life."

"I reckon dat's so; but I must be goin' back after Miss Elsie and de res'," said Solon, pick-

ing up his hat and putting it on as he passed
out into the grounds.

His story caused great excitement at Roselands, and the whole Ion family, with their
guests, hastened home in anxiety to hear the
version of the story Edward and Herbert would
give, and to learn what had been the effect of
the fright upon Zoe and the babies.

Solon's report was: "Miss Zoe she scared most
to deff, and Mr. Ed'ard he huggin' her up, and
comfortin' her all de way home; an' she's afraid
of de trees on de lawn at Ion, les' dey falls sud-
dent—like de one in de woods—and kill somebody. But Mr. Ed'ard he tells her to trust
in de Lawd, an' she needn't be 'fraid ob
nothin'."

"And the babies, Solon?" asked Rosie;
"weren't they frightened almost into fits?"

"Not a bit, Miss Rosie," returned Solon,
chuckling; "dey's just 'sprised, dey was, an'
quiet as two little mouses. 'Spect dey's won-
derin' what makes deir mudder cry so, and
deir fader hug her and dem up so tight."

"Ah, here comes Herbert," said Harold, who,
with Croly, was riding alongside of the carriage.
"We'll get the whole story from him."

"Ah, has Solon been telling you of our ad-
venture in the woods this evening?" asked Herbert, reining in his steed near at hand. "It

was quite an exciting one, and we have great reason for gratitude over our narrow escape."

"As we all have," returned his mother with emotion. "It was you, Herbert, was it not, who saw the tree tottering and gave warning to the others?"

"Yes, mother. I, being on horseback, had of course a much better opportunity to see it than the others in the covered carriage; yet it was a good Providence that turned my eyes in that direction at that precise moment, and thus saved, possibly, all our lives."

"Oh, we can never be thankful enough for that!" exclaimed his mother. "But Zoe was very much frightened, Solon says?"

"Oh, very much, and no wonder, poor thing! But Edward took her and the babies directly to their rooms, and I have not seen them since. I wrote my letter, rode in to Union and mailed it, and have just ridden out again."

The carriage had been at a standstill while they talked, but now Mrs. Travilla bade Solon drive on. They were very near home, and in another minute or two had turned in at the avenue gates.

Edward was waiting on the veranda to assist them to alight, and his mother at once inquired anxiously about Zoe and the twins.

"The little ones are asleep, and Zoe is resting

pretty quietly now on her couch," Edward replied. "I suppose Herbert and Solon have told you of our narrow escape from being crushed by a falling tree as we passed through that bit of woods?"

"Yes; it was a wonderful escape," Elsie returned in tones quivering with emotion. "I can never be thankful enough for the spared lives of my children. Would Zoe care to see her mother just now, do you think?"

"Yes, yes, indeed, mother! Shall I take you to her now? Our guests will excuse us, I know, and we will leave the others to entertain them."

Zoe, lying on the couch in her dressing-room, the crib with its sleeping little occupants within reach of her hand, started up with a glad cry, "O mamma, dear mamma, how glad I am to see you!" as her husband and his mother came softly in and drew near where she lay.

Elsie took her in her arms and held her close with low-breathed words of tenderness and love. "My dear girl! my dear daughter! thank God that I have you safe in my arms again. How little I thought of such danger when we parted an hour ago, and oh! to have lost you—my sons—Edward and Herbert, and the darling babies, or any one of you!—ah, it is almost too terrible to think of for a moment."

"Yes, mamma dear; even the sudden dan-

ger, though we all escaped, gave me a shock
that has completely unnerved me. I cannot
forget for a moment how near we were to death
—so sudden and dreadful—escaping only as by
the skin of our teeth."

She shuddered and was silent for a moment,
still clinging to her mother, and held fast in
her loving embrace; then in a low, sweet voice,
"Mamma, dearest mamma," she said, "this
terrible experience, this narrow escape from a
sudden, awful death, has proved to me a blessing in disguise. I have given myself to God
and feel that he has taken me for his very own
child; and oh, amid all my suffering from shat-
tered nerves, there is a sweet peace in my heart
such as I have never known before!"

"My dear, dear child!" Elsie exclaimed with
emotion, "no sweeter, no gladder tidings could
have reached me. It is an answer to prayer
offered for years that you—my Edward's wife
—might learn to know and love the Lord who
shed his own precious blood that we might have
eternal life."

"Yes, mamma, I wonder at myself that I
could have ever resisted such love, that I did
not give him my whole heart years ago, and
strive to serve him with all my powers."

"Yes, dear little wife," Edward said with
emotion, "what seemed to us so terrible at

the time has turned out a real blessing in disguise."

"So may every trial prove to you, my dear children," said his mother. "I must leave you now; and Zoe dear, go to sleep in peace, fearing no evil. Remember and rest upon those sweet words: 'The Lord is thy keeper; the Lord is thy shade upon thy right hand. The sun shall not smite thee by day, nor the moon by night. The Lord shall preserve thee from all evil; he shall preserve thy soul.'"

Edward saw his mother to the door and kissed her good-night.

"My dear boy, I am very glad for you," she said, "glad that you and your young wife, the mother of your babes, are at last travelling the same road, and may hope to spend a blest eternity together."

"Yes, mother dear, I think I have great reason to thank God for that narrow escape of ours from a sudden, terrible death," he replied in tones tremulous with emotion. "It was better than not to have been in danger, since it has proved to be the means of opening Zoe's eyes to her guilt and danger as a sinner who had never sought pardon and safety in the one way God has provided."

"Yes, my heart sings for joy for her and for you. But she is quite worn out; get her to

13

minutes' ride or drive from the village if one has the right kind of steed."

"Ah, you think of going into business in Union, do you?" inquired the captain in a tone of surprise.

"Yes, I have been quietly spying out the land," replied Cousin Ronald, "and if Hugh agrees with me in thinking it a suitable place for a factory, I think we shall buy and build there."

"That is a pleasant prospect for us," said Captain Raymond. "If you like, I will drive you both over there to-morrow and also take you to look at Beechwood."

The offer was at once accepted with thanks, and dismissing his pupils a little earlier than usual the next morning, the captain fulfilled his promise to his guests.

When they returned, the news they brought was that they had secured a suitable site for a factory in the outskirts of Union, and were carrying on negotiations for the purchase of Beechwood.

"But who is going to keep house for you, Cousin Ronald?" asked Lulu.

"Marian, I hope," replied the old gentleman, looking smilingly at her. "You can do that in addition to attending to your studies, can you not, my bonny lassie?"

"I can try," she said with a look of delight; "for oh, but it would be pleasant to have a home with my dear, kind old kinsman."

"And so near to us, Marian. I hope you are as glad of that as I am," exclaimed Lulu.

"Oh, yes, yes, indeed!" cried Marian. "I hope there will be seldom a day when we shall not see each other; for you are like a sister to me."

"And you will come here to recite every school day, I hope," said the captain, "for I do not want to lose so painstaking, industrious, and promising a pupil."

"Nor I so good and kind a teacher," responded Marian, looking her thanks.

"I am much pleased with the place and its near vicinity to this one, the home of kind and congenial relatives," remarked Hugh Lilburn, "but as yet we are not entirely sure of securing it. You know the old saying, 'There's many a slip 'twixt the cup and the lip.'"

"Very true, laddie," said his father, "yet in this case I feel little apprehension of failure."

"Do you not like the house, Cousin Hugh?" asked Marian.

"It suits me nicely," he replied, "and I think you can hardly fail to like it. The grounds too are to my taste. I think if we are successful in securing it, it will make us a delightful home."

By the next evening he was able to say they had secured it, and would get possession in a fortnight. Marian and Lulu were full of delight, and indeed every one seemed much pleased.

" Will you move in as soon as the other folks are out, Cousin Ronald?" asked Grace.

" We hope to do so," he replied. " However, we shall need to do some furnishing first. This is Saturday evening: Cousin Vi, do you think you and your mother could go with us to the city next Monday and help us make our selection?"

" Yes, indeed; I shall be delighted to do so, and I have no doubt mamma will gladly accompany us. Marian is to be one of the party, I suppose?"

" Oh, yes, if the captain will give her leave of absence for a few hours?"

" Certainly, for an occasion so important," the captain said pleasantly.

" If it were holiday time Lulu too should be invited to accompany us," remarked Mr. Lilburn, " and I hope there will be another time when she can."

" Thank you, sir, I should be glad to go along if it were not that I know papa wants me to stay at home and attend to lessons; and I don't want to miss them, as our holidays will soon begin."

"That's right, lassie," he said; "make good use of your fine opportunities, and learn all you can in these young days that you may be the better prepared for usefulness in future years."

"Yes, sir; that is just what papa often says to us," replied Lulu, with a loving smile up into her father's face; "and I've found out that he always knows best about whatever concerns me."

"Quite a fortunate discovery for you," returned Mr. Lilburn with a kindly smile, while the captain's look was full of gratified approval.

"My dear little daughter," he said when he came to bid her good-night in her room, "your willingness to stay at home and attend to lessons instead of going to the city to help Marian with her shopping pleases me very much, because it shows that you have confidence in your father's wisdom and his love for you."

He smoothed her hair caressingly and kissed her as he spoke.

"Thank you for telling me that, you dear papa," she returned, her eyes shining. "I know you love me, and that your requirements are always meant for my good; also that you are very wise and know what is best for your own little girl. Oh, I'm so glad I am your very own!" she added, hugging him with all her strength.

"Not gladder than I am to own you, my darling," he said, repeating his caress. "I should like to give you the pleasure of going were it not that I feel that you have had already more interruptions to your studies than ought really to have been allowed."

"Yes, papa, I believe I have," she returned, "and as I do want to be as well educated as possible, so that I may be very useful if God spares my life, I really do not want you to indulge me more in play-times and holidays than you think best."

# CHAPTER XIV.

THE next day was the Sabbath, and spent as that holy day usually was by our friends at Ion, Woodburn, and by their near kindred on the neighboring estates. To Zoe, rejoicing in her new hope—the blessed hope that she was indeed a child of God and an heir of glory—it was a sweetly solemn and happy day, and to her young husband almost equally so. They attended church in company with the other members of the family and received many kindly greetings and inquiries in regard to the narrow escape of Thursday night.

Grace Raymond seemed very thoughtful on the homeward drive. "Papa," she asked at length, "do trees often fall suddenly like that one that came so near killing Aunt Zoe and the rest?"

"I think not very often, daughter," he replied. "I have heard of only one other such occurrence. Some years ago, out in Wisconsin, two little girls, sisters, were walking along near the edge of one of those pretty little lakes of

"No, little sister, it was rather that you were wanted in the school-room," replied the captain with a slightly amused look. "Now let us all go there, and perhaps we may pick up something more valuable than we could have found in the city stores."

"I think perhaps we may, papa," Grace said with a bright, pleased look and slipping her hand into his.

"I think so too, papa, and mean to try my very best," said Lulu, taking possession of his other hand and moving on with him and Grace in the direction of the school-room, Rosie and Walter following.

Rosie's vexation was all pretence; she set diligently to work, as did each of the others, and all went swimmingly with them and their teacher till the day's tasks were done and they dismissed to their sports.

Rosie and Walter had permission to stay at Woodburn until their mother's return, which was not till near tea-time. So they dined with the captain and his children, and they were a very merry little party, the captain jesting with them all in a way to both entertain the older ones and help the babies to forget their mother's absence.

They seemed to do so, and to be content and happy with their father and sisters, yet when mamma returned to them received her with demonstrations of delight.

Both the captain and Violet urged Grandma Elsie to stay to tea, keeping Rosie and Walter there with her.

"We want a little visit from you, mother," added the captain; "would be very glad to have you stay all night and as much longer as you will, but our family carriage will be at your service to carry you to Ion whenever you desire to go."

"Yes, mamma, do stay at least till after tea," urged Walter; "it is very pleasant here, about as pleasant as at home, and I think the change may be of benefit to you."

"So you are turning doctor, are you, Walter?" laughed Rosie. "It might be well to engage Cousin Art to superintend your studies as well as those of Harold and Herbert; though it seems to me it would be rather a mistake to put so many lads out of one family into one profession."

"That is a question that may be considered at some other time," returned Walter, with unmoved gravity. "Mamma, you will stay, will you not?"

"Yes, since a visit here is the prescription of my little new doctor," Elsie returned with a smile; "and since the host and hostess are both so kindly urgent."

you not?" asked Grandma Elsie, turning to him.

"I think not, cousin," he replied. "I want to be here to help my laddie with his building and the adorning of the house that's to make a home for Marian here and ourselves," smiling kindly upon his young relative as he spoke. "But I quite approve of her accompanying you, for she's been a diligent scholar, the captain tells me, and occasional rest and diversions are very good and desirable things for the young."

"No better than for the old, Cousin Ronald," returned Marian with a grateful, loving look into his eyes; "and if you don't need them I do not, I am sure. I've had a very great change of scene and life, and a long journey too, within the last few months, you know, and now there is nothing I should enjoy more than staying here and helping you to put the new home in order and place the pretty furniture we bought to-day."

Cousin Ronald and Hugh both looked much pleased with her choice.

"Ah, lassie, you appreciate your privileges," said Mr. Lilburn, "which is more than can be said of everybody."

"But everybody has not so many privileges or so great as mine," returned Marian, her eyes shining.

## CHAPTER XV.

THE captain's pupils were jubilant over the prospect of soon leaving for the sea-shore at the North. Inquiries in regard to different locations had been set on foot some weeks previous, and now it was decided to take possession for the season of several dwellings in the neighborhood of Cape Ann, Mass. In one of them, which was quite large, too large to be called a cottage, the Ion and Woodburn families would be together much of the time, a little building near at hand containing the overflow when guests would render accommodations at the larger house too small.

Edward and Zoe with their little ones would remain at home for the present, that he might oversee the work on the plantation, and the Fairview family would go for a time at least to Evelyn's home on the banks of the Hudson. The families at the Oaks and the Laurels were not going North at present, but might do so later in the season.

The Raymonds were to take their journey by sea in the *Dolphin*, the others, with their guests, going by rail.

That was the plan at first, but only a day or two before they started Mary Keith received a letter from her father giving her permission to accept an invitation from the relatives to spend the summer with them at the sea-shore, which she did with delight.

"Oh, I am so glad, Mary!" Violet exclaimed when she heard the news; "and I want you to go with us on the *Dolphin*. Won't you? It will be a new and, I hope, pleasant experience for you, and we shall be so glad to have your company."

Captain Raymond, who was present, warmly seconded the invitation, and Mary accepted it.

This talk was at Ion, where the captain and Violet were making a short call. They took their leave almost immediately, saying that the time for their preparations for leaving home was growing very short, and there were a number of matters still claiming their attention.

Before they had reached the avenue gates the captain turned to his wife, saying, "I think, my dear, if you have no objection, we will drive over to Roselands for a short call before going home. I want to say a few words to Cal."

There was a twinkle of fun in his eye, and

Violet returned laughingly, "Yes, I understand. Let us go by all means."

On reaching Roselands they did not alight, but said to Calhoun, who came out to welcome them, that they were in haste, only wanted a few words with him, and then must return home.

"Yes," he said; "you leave day after tomorrow, I believe? Is there something you would like me to attend to for you in your absence, captain?"

"No, thank you," was the smiling reply; "what we want is to take you with us. You have not taken a holiday for years; we have plenty of room for you on the yacht, and can assure you of pleasant company—the very pleasantest you could have, for Cousin Mary Keith has consented to go with us."

"And you think that furnishes an additional inducement?" Calhoun returned, coloring and laughing. "Well, I won't deny that it does. But this is very sudden."

"You needn't decide at once; talk it over with Art, and we shall hope you will decide to go. We shall be glad to take you as a passenger, though it should be at the last minute. Goodmorning;" and with the last word the carriage started down the avenue.

Arthur called that evening to thank the cap-

tain for the invitation to Calhoun and say that
it would be accepted.

"He really needs a rest," he said, "and though
I had some difficulty in persuading him that
he could be done without for a few weeks, I
succeeded at last, though a bit of information
about a certain passenger," he added with a
smile, "had probably more to do with his ac-
ceptance than anything else."

"O Cousin Arthur, I wish you could go too!"
exclaimed Violet. "Don't you think you
could?"

"Yes, can't you?" asked the captain. "We
should be delighted to have you, for the sake of
your pleasant company, to say nothing of the
convenience of having our medical adviser close
at hand in case of sickness or accident."

"Thank you kindly," returned the doctor.
"I should greatly enjoy going, especially in such
pleasant company, but it would not do for Cal
and me to absent ourselves at one and the same
time. Besides, I have some patients that I
could not leave just at present."

"Then take your turn after Calhoun comes
home," said the captain. "He would be a
welcome guest as long as he might choose to
stay, but if I know him as I think I do, he is
not likely to stay as long as we do."

"No, not he," said Arthur; "if he stays two

or three weeks it will be quite as much as I expect."

"And we shall hope to see you after that," said the captain. "Don't forget that 'all work and no play makes Jack a dull boy,' and we could ill afford to have our doctor so transformed."

"Many thanks," returned Arthur. "I sometimes feel that such a rest would do me a world of good, and perhaps prevent or delay such a catastrophe as you speak of," he added with a smile; "but it is really a very difficult thing for a busy country doctor to get away from his work for even a brief holiday."

"Yes, but I think he should take one occasionally nevertheless," said the captain; "since by so doing he is likely to last the longer, and in the end do more for his fellow-creatures."

"Very pleasant doctrine, captain," laughed Arthur. "But I must be going now, as some of these same fellow-creatures are in need of my services at this present moment."

"I wish you were going with us now, Art," said Violet as she bade him good-by. "It would be really delightful to have you along as friend and relative as well as physician."

"That is very good and kind in you," he returned. "I won't forget it, and perhaps I may look in on you before the summer is over."

That day and the next were very busy ones at Woodburn and Ion, and the succeeding one saw them all on their way northward. Mary Keith was delighted with the yacht, which she had not seen until she boarded it in company with the Raymonds. It was a pleasure to Violet to take her cousin down into the cabin and show her all its beauties and conveniences, including the state-room she was to occupy on the voyage.

"Oh, how lovely!" cried Mary; "and how good in you to ask me to go with you in this beautiful vessel. I am sure the journey will not be half so wearisome as it would in the cars."

"I hope not," returned Violet, "but I hope you won't be sea-sick; for if you are you will probably wish we had not induced you to try the voyage in preference to the journey by land."

"And perhaps that you had my doctor brother as fellow-passenger instead of myself," remarked a familiar voice behind them—that of Calhoun Conly—and turning quickly they discovered him and the captain standing near by, regarding them with amused, smiling countenances.

"Welcome! I'm glad to see you, Cal," said Violet, holding out her hand.

"Thank you, Vi," he returned, taking the

hand in a cordial grasp. "And you, Miss Mary, are not displeased, I hope, that I have accepted an invitation to join your party on the voyage and for a short time at the sea-shore."

"No, Mr. Conly," laughed Mary. "Whom the captain and Violet choose to invite is, I am sure, no affair of mine; nor should I object to your company so long as you continue so inoffensive as you have been during our brief acquaintance."

"Thanks," he returned, bowing low; "now I feel entirely comfortable."

"That's right, Cal," said the captain. "And suppose we all go on deck to see the weighing of the anchor and the starting of the vessel; for the steam is up and we are about ready to move."

An awning shaded the deck and a breeze from the sea made it a pleasant place to lounge and read or chat. The children were already seated there, watching the movements of the sailors and of the people on the wharf.

"How d'y do, Cousin Cal?" said Lulu, making room for him and Mary Keith on the settee she had been occupying. "I'm glad you are going with us, and I hope you and Cousin Mary will have a good time, for I think a journey taken on the *Dolphin* is very much more enjoyable than one by rail."

"I have no doubt of it—if one is not attacked by sea-sickness," returned Calhoun.

"Are you likely to be?" she asked.

"Well, that I cannot tell, as this will be my first voyage," he answered.

"As it is mine," said Mary.

"If you are both sick you can sympathize each with the other," remarked Violet laughingly.

But the captain had walked forward to give his orders, the work of weighing anchor was beginning, and all kept silence while watching it. Presently the vessel was speeding on her way, and they had nothing to do but sit under the awning enjoying the breeze and the prospect of the wide expanse of ocean on the one side and the fast-receding shore on the other.

The voyage proved a speedy and prosperous one, continuous fair weather and favorable winds making it most enjoyable. One pleasant afternoon they entered Gloucester harbor, and before night were safely housed in their new temporary home, where they found the Dinsmores and Travillas awaiting them.

Mr. Croly too was there to join in the greetings. Domiciled with relatives who occupied a cottage but a few rods distant, he passed much of his time with Harold and Herbert, fishing, boating, bathing, riding, or driving; pleasures that were now shared by the other gentlemen and ladies and more or less by the children also; the captain, young uncles, and occasionally Mr. Croly caring for them when in bathing and seeing that they had a fair share of the pleasures of the older people.

There were many beautiful drives to be taken, some interesting spots to visit. One day they took a long drive, much of it through a pleasant wood, whence they emerged within a few hundred yards of the sea-shore, there very high and rocky. They fastened their horses in the edge of the wood, alighted, and walked out in the direction of the sound of the dashing, booming waves.

Stepping across a narrow fissure in the rocks, the gentlemen helping the ladies and children over, they could see that it widened toward the water and that the sea roared and foamed like a seething caldron about the base of the rocks, which were very steep and uneven, in many places great stones piled upon each other in a way that made them look as if it would take very little to send them toppling down into the roaring, fuming water below.

Grace clung to her father in affright. "O papa, please don't let us go any nearer," she said; "please hold me tight."

"I will, my darling," he answered soothingly. "We are in no danger here, and you can just stand and look, seeing all you need care to. Then I will take you back to mamma, over yonder where she is gathering flowers for Elsie and Ned, and you can stay with and amuse them while she comes here to take a look."

"Yes, I'd rather be there," she said, "for it seems so dangerous here. O papa, see! Lu is going so near the edge. I'm afraid she'll fall in."

"Uncle Harold has her hand," he said; "still I do not like to see her venturing so near the edge. Lucilla," he called, "come here, daughter."

She turned about and came at once. "Uncle Harold was taking care of me, papa," she said; "but oh, it does look dangerous, and I shouldn't like to go climbing about over the rocks as Cousin Mary and Rosie are doing; at least not unless I had you to hold me, papa."

"I shall not take you into any such dangerous place," he said, "nor will I allow any one else to do so. Do you see that little cross there?" pointing to a small wooden one driven in the rock near by.

"Yes, sir. What is it there for?" asked Lulu.

"As a reminder of a sad accident that happened here some years ago. A party of summer visitors to this coast came out here one day as we have done and went down near the waves. Among them was a very estimable young lady, a Christian, I believe she was, a teacher too, supporting her aged parents by her industry. She was soon to be married, and with her were the parents of her intended husband.

"It seems they all went down near the waves, this young lady nearer than the others. She seated herself on the rock against which the waves dash up. Some of the others called to her that she was not in a safe place, but she replied that she thought it safe; the waves did not come up close to her, and they looked away in another direction for a moment; when they turned to look for her again she was gone from the rock, and all they could see of her was one hand held up out of the boiling waves as if in a wild appeal for help. Help which they could not give, for they had no boat and no other way of reaching her."

"Was she drowned, papa?" asked Grace.

"Yes, my child; she could not live many minutes amid such waves and rocks. They made all the haste they could to get help, but none was near at hand, and she must have been dead long before they got it there. They did get the body finally, with grappling irons, but the soul had fled.

"My children, remember what I say to you now. Never run the risk of losing your lives when nothing is to be gained by it for either yourselves or others; to do so is both wrong and foolish; it is really breaking the sixth commandment—'Thou shalt not kill.' We have no right to kill ourselves, not even to escape great suffering, but must wait God's time to call us hence.

"Now I will take you to your little sister and brother, to take charge of them while your mamma comes to view Rafe's Chasm."

In the mean time Grandma Elsie had called to Rosie and Walter, and was talking to them, in much the same strain, of the folly and sinfulness of unnecessarily exposing themselves to danger.

"You can see almost as much from this safe place as you can by going into those very dangerous ones," she said. Then she told them the same story the captain had just been telling his little girls.

"O mamma, how dreadful, how very dreadful!" exclaimed Rosie; "it was so sad to be snatched away from life so suddenly, while young and well and with so much to live for."

"Yes," sighed her mother; "my heart aches for the poor parents, even more than for the lover. He has probably found another bride before this, while they still mourn the irreparable loss of their dear daughter."

"Your mother is right, children," said Mr. Dinsmore, standing near. "Heed her teachings, and never risk life or limb in a mere spirit of bravado."

The captain now stood beside them with Violet on his arm, and the others came climbing back, till they all stood in a group together.

"What an awful occurrence that was! what a dreadful death to die—tossed about by those booming waves, that raging, foaming water, against those cruel rocks till life was extinct," Violet said, gazing down into the chasm while clinging tightly to her husband's arm.

"Yes," said Mary Keith, "and I feel that I was hardly right to run the risk I did in climbing about as I have been doing."

"Nor I," said Croly.

"Nor any of the rest of us," added Calhoun; "but we won't do it any more. But what is it Vi refers to? Has there ever been an accident here?"

"Yes; have you not heard the story?" said his uncle. "Has no one told you the meaning of yonder cross?" pointing to it as he spoke.

"No, sir; and I had not noticed it before."

Mr. Dinsmore briefly told the sad tale; then

"Yes, I am hoping every day to hear that they are about sailing; but I have heard nothing at all for some weeks, and am growing more anxious day by day. Aunt and uncle try to comfort and reassure me with the old saying that 'no news is good news,' but—well, my only comfort is in casting my cares on the Lord, remembering that he cares for both them and me, and that his promise is, 'As thy days, so shall thy strength be.'"

"That is one of my mother's favorite texts," remarked Herbert, "and she says it has always been fulfilled to her."

"And she has seen some sore trials?"

"Yes; my father's death for one. I know that was the greatest of all; though before that, death had snatched away from her a very dear and lovely little daughter," said Harold.

"And she has had trials in other forms," added Herbert. "Some persons would esteem it a very great trial to be called to choose between a difficult and dangerous surgical operation and certain, painful death from disease."

"And she has had that trial?" asked Croly.

"Yes; and went through it bravely, trusting in the Lord to spare her life or take her to dwell with him in bliss forever."

"She is a noble and lovely woman," remarked

Croly. "I never saw one whom I admired more."

"Ah, you do not know half how sweet and good, and what a devoted Christian she—our beloved mother—is," said Harold earnestly. "I thank God every day for giving me such a mother."

"As I do," said Herbert. "I often think if there is anything good in me, it is the result of my mother's kind, wise, loving training."

## CHAPTER XVI.

THE next day was the Sabbath—the third since the arrival of the Raymonds. Rain fell heavily. There was no church near at hand, and our friends gathered in the parlors of the house occupied by the Dinsmores, Travillas, and Raymonds, where a sermon was read, prayers were offered, and hymns sung. In the evening they held a Bible-reading, and afterward sang hymns, now selected or suggested by one, now by another.

Croly chose several. He had been with them in the morning and offered a very feeling, fervent prayer. The first two verses of the last hymn sung at his request were:

"My days are gliding swiftly by,
    And I, a pilgrim stranger,
Would not detain them as they fly,
    These hours of toil and danger.
For oh, we stand on Jordan's strand,
    Our friends are passing over,
And, just before, the shining shore
    We may almost discover.

"Our absent King the watch-word gave,
  'Let every lamp be burning;'
We look afar across the wave,
  Our distant home discerning.
For oh, we stand on Jordan's strand,
  Our friends are passing over,
And, just before, the shining shore
  We may almost discover."

Monday was a bright, beautiful day, spent by
our friends very much as usual. They had
been unusually long without letters from their
homes or that vicinity, and were growing a
trifle anxious; Calhoun in especial, as he felt
that he himself had had a good vacation, and
it was time that his brother, the doctor, was
taking his turn. Yet there was a very strong
tie binding him for the present to the spot
where he was. He and Mary Keith had come
to an understanding and were mutual lovers,
only awaiting the consent of her parents to become engaged. He had written to Mr. Keith,
telling him frankly of his circumstances and
prospects, his love for Mary, and desire to make
her his wife at the earliest day on which her
parents could be induced to resign her to him,
also of her willingness to become his; concluding his letter by a reference to their cousin and
his uncle, Mr. Dinsmore, for any desired information in regard to his character and the

correctness of his statements concerning his ability, present and prospective, to support a wife and family.

He and Mary walked out that morning soon after breakfast, strolled along the beach for a time, then seated themselves within sight of their temporary home.

They had hardly done so, when Walter Travilla came running with letters which he said had just come from the office.

"There are several for each of you; you are fortunate this morning," he added; "however, that depends very much upon what is in them."

"So it does, Wal," said Calhoun, glancing at his, and perceiving that the direction on one of them was in a masculine hand and the post-mark that of the town where Mary's parents lived.

His pulses quickened at the sight, and his face flushed.

Walter had run away, and Mary was breaking the seal of her own letter from home; she seemed too busy with it to notice the excitement of her companion, seeing which he silently opened and read his to himself.

The two epistles were of much the same tone and tenor. The parents, though feeling it a sore trial to part with their child---their eldest daughter—gave full consent, since that seemed necessary to her happiness.

Mary's feelings as she read were of strangely mingled happiness and heartache. She loved the man at her side, loved him so dearly that she could scarce have borne to resign him, yet the thought of leaving the dear parents who had loved and cherished her all her days was almost equally unendurable. Her tears began to fall, and the sound of a low sob startled Calhoun just as he finished the perusal of Mr. Keith's letter, which brought only joy to him.

"Oh, dearest, what is it?" he asked, passing an arm about her waist. "Does that letter bring you bad news? Mine gives me only the joyful intelligence of your parents' consent; so that I have a right to comfort you in any trouble, if it lies in my power."

"Do not be vexed or offended that the same news is not all joy to me," she returned, smiling through her tears. "My father and mother are very, very dear to me; they have loved and cherished me all my life; their home has always been mine, and—" but overcome by emotion, she ended with a sob, leaving her sentence unfinished.

"And you are giving them up for me, a comparative stranger, and far from worthy of such a prize as yourself," he said in low, tender tones, taking her hand and pressing it affectionately in his. " Dear girl, if love, tenderness, entire devotion can make you happy, you shall never regret the sacrifice."

" I have no fear of that," she returned, smiling through her tears, " for though but a few weeks have passed since we first saw each other, you are well known to us through Uncle Dinsmore, Cousin Elsie, and others. I do not fear to trust you—oh, no, it is not that, but the leaving of the dear father and mother now— when they begin to grow old and may need a daughter's care."

" But they have other daughters?"

" Yes, but I am the eldest, and the one who would perhaps know best how to make them comfortable."

" Well, dearest, let us leave that for the present. There is plenty of room at Roselands, and perhaps—should your father some day retire from business—they may like to come and make their home with us. If so, we shall be glad, very glad to have them."

That was a word of comfort that chased Mary's tears away, and the rest of their talk was gay and happy; the principal subject their plans for the immediate future.

" I ought to be going home," remarked Calhoun at length, with a slight sigh, " though the fact is I don't know how to tear myself away. But I must, for poor, overworked Art must have his turn. Ah, here's a letter from him," taking up one from the still unexamined, half-forgotten pile lying on the grass by his side

Hastily tearing it open, he glanced over the contents. "Why, here is news!" he exclaimed. "Marian McAlpine has been quite ill, Art attending her; she's convalescing, but needs change of climate and scene. Art has prescribed a few weeks at the sea-shore, and they are coming here—the whole four of them—Mr. Lilburn and his son, Miss Marian, and Art as her attending physician. I am commissioned to find a boarding-place for them. But what are they thinking of? They were to start the day after this was written, and will probably be here to-night or to-morrow. Oh, well, there are hotels in the town, and I must just hurry in there, make inquiries, and do the best I can for them."

"Yes; let us go back to the house at once," said Mary. "But ah, here comes Cousin Elsie," she added, as they both rose and turned toward the dwelling.

"You had a letter from Art, I noticed, Calhoun," said Mrs. Travilla, hastening toward them, "and I presume it brings the same news as this one from Cousin Ronald to me," indicating one that she held in her hand. "He says Marian has been really very ill, but is convalescing, and they are bringing her here, thinking the sea-air may do her good. He says Arthur is coming along as her physician, but agrees with him that it is not at all necessary for you to hurry home, as Edward is able and willing to give some little attention to the workers on your plantation."

"That is good news," Calhoun said with a smile, "but I must hurry into the city and find a boarding-place for them."

"Why, Cal, you astonish me!" exclaimed Elsie. "Have I ever shown myself so inhospitable that you have a right to suppose I would let relatives go to a hotel when I can make room for them in my home?"

"I didn't think you could, cousin," he returned.

"I both can and will, if I am allowed the opportunity; it is only a little crowding that is necessary. Mr. Conly can take his brother the doctor into his room to share his bed, Cousin Ronald and his son can share another—and there is a spare room waiting for them—while Marian can be taken in with some of us. I have not thought it all out yet, but am confident I can soon arrange it."

"Oh, easily, cousin," said Mary, "for Rosie

and I could easily take Lulu or Grace, or both of them, into our room. Crowding at the seashore is nothing new, and I do not think it will be at all unpleasant to me."

"You are a dear, good girl, Mary," was Elsie's smiling response as she turned and hastened back to the house.

"She has her full share of the Southern virtue of hospitality," remarked Calhoun, looking after her with admiring eyes.

"Do you consider it a specially Southern virtue?" queried Mary with a little laugh of amusement.

"I beg your pardon," returned Calhoun gallantly, "and acknowledge that I have seen no lack of the virtue in question since coming up North, but I have always heard it spoken of as particularly characteristic of my native section of the Union, though I dare say that is altogether a mistake."

"I shall try to convince you of that one of these days," she said with a smiling look up into his eyes.

When Mrs. Travilla reached the house, there was first a short consultation among the older members of the family, then a pleasant little bustle of preparation for the expected, welcome guests, who it was found could be easily accommodated without greatly disturbing or interfering with the comfort of any one else.

These preparations completed, all gathered on the porch and sat there, the gentlemen reading, the ladies crocheting or merely chatting to pass away the time till the dinner-bell should summon them to the table. But a carriage was seen approaching from the direction of the town.

" I wonder, now, if it isn't our party," said Calhoun, and even as he spoke it drove up and stopped before the gate; seeing which he, Harold, and Herbert sprang up and hastened forward to assist the travellers to alight; for it was indeed the expected party of relatives from the South.

The gentlemen were all well and in fine spirits, but Marian was much exhausted and glad to be taken directly to bed. The doctor seemed very careful of his patient, the other two equally solicitous for her comfort; as were Mrs. Dinsmore, Elsie, and Violet, all of whom were ready to do for her anything in their power.

All she wanted, however, was a little light nourishment, then a long sound sleep, and the next morning she was able to occupy a hammock swung upon the porch, where she passed her time listening to reading, generally by the doctor, who rarely left her long for the first day or two, chatting with the cousins or sleeping; weakness and the sea-air having somewhat the effect of an opiate.

But both the air and the sleep did her great good, so that in a few days she was able to take short drives and even walks along the beach with the support of the arm of one or another of the gentlemen, oftener that of Arthur than any other. He watched over her with the care and tenderness of a mother, noticed the first sign of exhaustion, and it was always he who helped her up the stairs to her bedroom, not infrequently half-carrying her there.

All the older members of the family noticed his devotion and quietly remarked upon it among themselves.

"He is really in love with her, I think, but it seems to me the disparity of years is too great," remarked Herbert one day when the matter was under discussion.

"Perhaps, laddie, when you come to be of his age you may see such matters in a different light," said Mr. Lilburn in a fatherly tone and with a kindly smile at his young relative.

"As his mother did before him," added Elsie, laying her hand affectionately in that of Herbert, who was as usual close at her side.

"Ah, mamma dear, I quite forgot at the

moment that you had married one so much older than yourself. But my father was no common man."

"No, nor is Cousin Arthur; at least so we all think, we to whom he has always been so kind and faithful as both relative and physician."

"Yes," said Mr. Dinsmore, "and any one who is so fortunate as to win his heart and hand will have one of the best, most affectionate, and attentive of husbands."

"And the disparity of years will not be so very much greater than between Cousin Mary and his brother," remarked Mrs. Dinsmore.

"And they seem a delightfully happy pair; as a certain married couple of my acquaintance, between whom there must be something like the same disparity of years, are to my actual knowledge," remarked Violet with a bright, fond look up into her husband's face as he sat by her side with baby Ned on his knee.

"Quite true, my dear. I could not be induced to exchange my one little wife for half a dozen women of twice her years, even if the law allowed it," returned the captain with a humorous look and smile.

"Nor could I be induced to exchange my one good big husband for a dozen or more other men of any age, size, or quality," laughed Violet.

"Wise Vi," remarked Herbert; "one is plenty; more than one would certainly be a superfluity. There—look toward the shore, everybody. Yonder are Cal and his beloved wandering together near the waves, seemingly in close conversation, while Art and his sit side by side on two camp-chairs a little nearer here, or a trifle farther from the water. There is certainly a good deal of love-making going on."

"At least things have that appearance," Harold said with a quiet smile as he and the others followed Herbert's advice, and gazing out seaward had a pretty view of the two pairs of lovers.

There was little doubt in any of their minds that Arthur and Marian belonged in that class, while the other two were openly acknowledged as such.

But they were somewhat mistaken. Arthur had not yet breathed a word of love to his young patient, and she thought of him only as her dear, kind doctor, who had done much to relieve her sufferings and had in all probability saved her life. She had strong confidence in his skill and was a perfectly tractable and obedient patient. He assisted her to her room that evening, as usual, more than an hour before any but the younger children were ready to retire.

It was a beautiful moonlight evening, and the porches, where most of the family were gathered, looked very inviting as he came down again and stepped out upon the one that ran along the front of the house.

His Cousin Elsie invited him to an easy-chair by her side, then presently proposed that they two should stroll around the porches together. He caught gladly at the suggestion, rose and offered her his arm.

" I want a little private chat with you, Art," she said, smiling brightly up into his face.

" I am always glad to talk with you, cousin," he returned, giving her an affectionate yet keenly scrutinizing look, " but I hope it is not of any serious ailment you have to tell me."

" Oh, no! I am thankful to be able to say that I and all my near and dear ones are in perfect health so far as I know. It is of yourself and your dear young patient I would speak. Marian is a sweet girl, lovely in both character and person."

" So I think. Ah, cousin, if I were only some years younger!"

" Never mind that, Art; you are young in looks and feeling, and I doubt if there is any one nearer and dearer to her now than yourself. She thinks her feeling for you is only the gratitude and affection any patient might feel for a kind, attentive, sympathizing physician, but I am much mistaken if on hearing the story of your love from your lips she will fail to discover that she loves you as a woman should the man to whom she gives her hand."

"Do you really think so, cousin?" he asked with a bright, glad smile.

"I do indeed," she replied, "and if I were in your place I should soon put it to the proof by offering her my hand and heart."

He seemed lost in thought for a moment, then heaving a sigh, "Ah, if I were only sure," he said—"sure of not, by so doing, losing the place I can see that I have already won in her heart—the friendship—it may not, after all, be anything more than that—I should not for a moment hesitate to make the offer you recommend; for I feel confident that with mutual love we might be exceptionally happy despite the difference in our years."

"No doubt of it," she returned, "and I hope that before you leave us you will put it to the proof; because I think it will be for both your happiness and hers."

"Thank you very much for both your sympathy and advice, dear cousin," he said. "I shall do so to-morrow if opportunity offers, as is likely to be the case, seeing we are so frequently alone together as patient and physician.

16

Then if I find she does not and cannot love me in the way I wish, I shall trouble her no longer with my presence, but speedily set off for home and its duties."

"But even in that case you need not entirely despair," his cousin said with a bright, sweet look up into his rather anxious and troubled face, "for she is but young, and clever courting may win her heart in time. You are such a dear fellow, Art, so kind-hearted, generous, sympathetic, so unselfish and helpful, that you seem to me to deserve every good thing in life."

"Oh, Cousin Elsie, such extravagant praise mortifies me, because I must acknowledge to myself that it is so far beyond my deserts," he returned, blushing like a girl.

"It need not," she said. "There is an old saying that every one—every deserving one at least—eats white bread at some time in his or her life. You have had a hard life so far, but I hope your time for white bread is now close at hand."

He laughed a little at that. "Yes," he said, "Cal and I have worked very hard for years past, and times do grow easier with us, but whether I shall ever get so far with the white bread as to win the dear young wife I covet, I do not know."

"Well, you have my best wishes," she returned, "and I shall do what I can to help the prosperity of your suit by sounding your praises in the ears of your lady-love. Ah, do not look alarmed, but trust me to say only enough to interest her, not so much as to weary her of the subject."

"Thank you, dear cousin, I know I can trust you fully. And will you not help me with your prayers that I may, if it be God's will, succeed in winning her heart completely?"

"Surely I will," she said, "and I believe our joint petition will be granted, if it be for the best."

Arthur lay awake for some time that night, pondering on Elsie's advice in regard to his contemplated suit for Marian's hand and asking divine guidance and help.

The next morning, soon after breakfast, he, as usual, asked Marian if she would like to go down on the beach and get a breath of the refreshing breeze from the sea.

"Yes, indeed, doctor, if it will not be keeping you from going somewhere with somebody else," she answered with a smile.

"Not at all," he returned. "I have no engagement, and shall be glad not only to help you to a breath of sea-air, but to take one myself."

He brought a light shawl and wrapped it about her, saying the breeze was rather fresh

tones, "forget the sweetest words I ever had
spoken to me? Oh, no, no! But I don't know
how you can give such love to me—a poor, ignorant girl, whose own father cares so little for her
that he would sacrifice her happiness for life."

"No, no," he said, gathering her in his arms,
"the sweetest, dearest, loveliest one that ever
crossed my path. And you can love me. Ah,
darling, you have made me the happiest of men;
you do not deny that you love me; and you are
to me the dearest of all earthly creatures."

He held her close, while she dropped her
head on his breast and wept for very joy and
thankfulness. For Elsie was right; he had
won her heart and was dearer to her than all
the world besides.

Many low-breathed, comforting, endearing
words fell from his lips as he held her close in
such loving embrace as she had not felt since
her mother's death, till at length her tears
ceased to fall and she was able to speak again.

"Oh, I never dreamed," she said, "that one
so wise and good could ever care in that way
for me. My heart is so full of joy and gratitude
to God and to you that words would not express
the half of it. But are you not afraid that you
may some day weary of a companion for life
who knows so much less than you do that she is
but a child in comparison with you?"

"Ah, no," he answered with a smile; "I have only feared that your youth and my years might stand in the way of my winning you; that a girl so sweet, fresh, and young would feel herself thrown away upon a man of my age. It would be but natural that you should prefer a much more youthful and finer-looking man."

"I do not know where I could find a finer-looking one," she answered with an earnest sincerity that made him smile. "Your face is so benevolent in expression, so full of goodness and kindness, that I could not help loving and trusting you from the first."

"Ah, darling, those are sweet words," he said, his eyes shining. "And you I found so patient and uncomplaining under suffering, so grateful for any and every kindness done you, every effort to give you relief, that I could but admire and end by loving you as I never loved before. Ah, dearest, that you return my love and have given yourself to me has made me the happiest of men! What a joy it will be to have you for my very own to love, cherish, and provide for!"

"And how sweet to me to belong to one who is so good and kind," she exclaimed, half-hiding her blushing face on his shoulder. "Oh, never before in all my life was I so happy as I am at this moment!"

my heart, hand, and fortune, which I offered her some days ago by letter."

At that there was a murmur of surprise from the listeners, accompanied by looks of pleasure; then the brothers shook hands with Hugh, wishing him joy and saying they should be glad to receive him into the family.

"My! what a lot of weddings we seem to be going to have!" exclaimed Rosie.   "I think I'll wait for mine till they are not quite such common affairs."

"Particularly as there's nobody offering to pair off with you yet, my pretty young sister," laughed Walter.   "I think, though, that the school-room is the best place for you and me for a while yet."

"Ah, Marian, here is a letter for you, my bonny lass; from your brother Sandy, I presume," said Mr. Lilburn, holding it out to her.

She took it eagerly, exclaiming, "Oh, yes, that is Sandy's writing!   The dear laddie! how I have wanted to hear from him."

"Read it, lass, and tell us if he says he will come to us, and if so how soon," said the old gentleman.

She hastened to obey, and presently announced in joyous tones, "Oh, yes, Cousin Ronald, he is delighted with your kind offer, and will come as soon as he has finished his present engagement, which will be in about a couple of months."

In the mean time Arthur had opened and read a letter handed him by his brother. He looked much pleased with its contents.

"Cousin Elsie," he said, "do you think you can accommodate me here a few days longer?"

"I am quite certain of it, provided you will stay," she answered with her own bright, sweet smile. "You need not have the slightest fear that you are not as welcome as the sunlight."

"Thank you very much," he said; "then I shall stay perhaps another week. This letter is from Cousin Dick Percival. He writes he has come there—to Roselands—for change of scene and air, as well as to see his relatives; can stay some weeks, and will take charge of my patients for a time, which he has in fact already begun to do."

"How nice!" exclaimed Rosie. "Dick is a good boy to enable us to keep you a little longer, and when you go back he will, I hope, come and pay a little visit here himself."

"Yes, I hope he will," said her mother. "I shall write and invite him to do so."

"Well, Cousin Art, I'm glad you are going to stay longer," said Walter, "but I hope none of us will be expected to get sick in order to give you employment."

members of the family had gone down to the
beach to be out of the way of those working
with Croly; but Rosie, Lulu, Grace, and Walter
were in a sad, subdued, and anxious mood.
Mary and Marian presently joined them, and
they talked feelingly of him whom they hardly
dared to hope to see in life again.

Yet all had great faith in Arthur's skill, and
the younger girls, telling of Harold's narrow
escape some years before at Nantucket, cheered
and encouraged the others with the hope that
Croly might even yet be saved from temporal
death, and live many years to be a comfort to
his parents and a blessing to the world.

"I do hope he is not gone and will live for
many years serving the Master here on earth,"
said Mary, "but if he is gone, we know that it
is to be with Jesus and forever blest. How he
loved that hymn about the shining shore! and
perhaps he has reached it now," she added with
a burst of tears.

"But oh, we will hope not! hope he is still
living and will be spared to the parents who
love him so dearly," said Marian. "And I believe if anybody can save him it is your cousin,
Dr. Conly."

"I'll run back to the house to see if there is
any sign of life yet," said Walter, and rushed
away.

He was back again in a few minutes, running, waving his handkerchief over his head, and showing so joyous a face that the others exclaimed half breathlessly, "Oh, is he coming to?"

"Yes, yes, Cousin Arthur says there are signs of life, and he thinks that he will be able to save him."

The glad news was received with a simultaneous burst of joyful exclamations.

"His parents have come," added Walter, "and are, oh! so anxious to see him, but don't know yet that anything is wrong with him."

And now with their minds relieved the girls were able to give attention to anything that might be going on within the range of their vision.

A boat was tied to the wharf and they saw that persons had left it and were wandering along the beach, among them an elderly man having several children in his care.

Presently this little group had seated themselves on the beach quite near our little party, and the smallest, a child of three, came toddling toward them.

"How do you do, baby girl? Do you like candy? Will you have a bite?" asked Rosie, holding out a tempting-looking morsel.

The little one stood gazing for a moment

with her finger in her mouth, then she accepted the offer.   "Dood!" she said smacking her lips. "Dot nudder bit for Sally?"

"Yes," Rosie said, bestowing another piece.

But another, older girl came running. "Sally," she said reprovingly, and seizing the little one's hand in an effort to draw her away, "you must not tease the ladies; papa says so. Come with me."

Sally resisted and Rosie said, "No, we are not teased.   We'd like to have her stay and talk to us."

But the father had come for his baby girl. "Please excuse her, young ladies," he said, lifting his hat politely, "she's pretty well spoiled. I've come to the seaside for a bit of rest and brought my children along, for I knew it would be quite a treat to them."

"And see, we've all got on the Union colors," said one of the little girls who had followed him, showing a rosette of red, white, and blue ribbon pinned to her dress.   "Father was a soldier in the war, and we all love the old flag."

"Oh, were you, sir?" cried Lulu delightedly. "Won't you please tell us of your experiences there?"

The other girls joined eagerly in the request, and at length, evidently pleased that they cared to hear the story, he sat down on the beach beside them and began it.

"In the war of the rebellion I was in the Shenandoah Valley with the infantry troops; a mere lad I was, only fifteen. One day I slipped off without leave, to visit an aunt living in Washington. We were at that time in camp on Georgetown Heights. Going back that night I lost my way and did not feel safe to ask it lest I should be thought a deserter; so finally went down into an area and, wearied out with my wanderings, fell asleep. It rained heavily through the night, but I was so weary and so used to hardship that I slept on and knew nothing about that till morning, when I waked to find myself lying in a puddle of water. I rose and hurried on my way; finally got back to camp, but so rheumatic from my wetting that I was sent to the hospital—in Washington. There my gun was taken from me and a receipt for it given me; so that when at length I recovered sufficiently to go back to camp, I was without a gun.

"It was not supplied to me immediately, and in the mean time the troops with whom I belonged were ordered to guard some wagons—a very long train—and while it was moving on, Mosby came up with his cavalry, took us prisoners, rifled the wagons of such things as he could carry away and use, and took the best horses for the use of his troops, leaving behind his own broken-down ones.

"Mosby's own troops and his prisoners were allowed to help themselves to such provisions as they could carry. I think they burnt all they could not take. When the rebs came upon us, one demanded my coat. I pulled it off and gave it to him; another took my hat, a third my shoes, so that I was not particularly well dressed when they were done with me.

"But I, as well as others, filled my haversack with provisions—hard-tack, pork, and so forth— and as they moved on each prisoner was obliged to lead one or more horses. I had but one.

"When the troops halted for the night the prisoners—among others—were ordered to take the horses to the river and water them. I had been all the time since my capture trying to contrive a way to escape. Now I saw a way, told a fellow-captive my plan, and asked him to render his aid by taking charge of my horse in addition to several already in his keeping. He consented. I slipped from the horse's back and, unobserved, got behind a large stone, allowed myself to sink in the water there till nearly covered—only able to breathe—and so remained till the troops of rebs and prisoners had left the spot.

"Then creeping cautiously out, I hurried on my way, going down the river bank, knowing the Union troops were camped somewhere lower down the stream.

"I trudged on all night, crept into the bushes and hid as day dawned—lying there all day tortured with heat and thirst as well as hunger—travelled on again the following night. Faint, weary, and worn with fatigue, hunger, and thirst, about nine o'clock seeing a light at a little distance I went toward it, feeling that I must venture for relief from my intolerable sufferings from hunger and thirst.

"As I drew near the light a dog began to bark from its vicinity and rushed out in my direction. At that I stood still and the dog came no nearer.

"But presently I heard the voice of a negro man asking: 'Who dar?' Knowing the negroes were always friends to the Union soldiers, I then came forward and told of my escape from the rebs and my desire to reach the Union camp, my ignorance of the right road, hunger, thirst, and weariness.

"The negro told me I was in a dangerous place—rebel troops being all about—and he and Dinah—his wife—had not much provision, but to come in and Dinah would give me something to eat, then I could go on my way, he showing me where to ford the river, the Federal troops being two or three miles farther down on the other side.

"I went with him into the cabin; an old negress greeted me kindly, and having heard my story undertook to get me some supper.

"She made a corn pone, took a pan with a division across the middle, put the pone in one side, some bacon in the other, and setting it on the coals, cooked them together, the fat from the bacon running through to the pone. It made as delicious a supper as I ever ate. She gave me a piece to carry along when I set out upon my journey again, as I did presently, travelling still farther down stream, till I reached a ford.

"Near there I lay down and slept soundly, not waking till the sun was two hours high.

"I was alarmed to find it so late, but I forded the river safely, and finally reached the Union camp.

"No one there knew me. I had not even a uniform to show what I was, so lest I might prove to be a spy I was ordered under arrest and confined till some of my own regiment who knew me came in and corroborated my story, or at least recognized me as one of themselves."

"That was a very interesting story, and we are much obliged to you for it, sir," said Lulu, as the narrator paused as if he had finished. "But can't you give us another?"

"Yes," he said, smiling in an absent-minded way. " I was just thinking of another and rather amusing occurrence that took place while I was a soldier, though it hadn't much to do with the war.

" My parents were living in Baltimore then, and I was still in the Shenandoah Valley. At one time, blackberries being very plenty in the woods where I was encamped, I gathered great quantities, filled a box, putting green leaves under and over the berries, nailed it up and sent it by express to my parents. I wrote to them about it, but the box started ahead of the letter and arrived first.

" In the mean time my mother and grand-mother had been talking of paying a visit to my older sister, who had married, was living in Philadelphia, and anxious and urgent to have them come on to see her and her first-born—a baby boy toddling about.

" They were most desirous to do so, as he was the first grandchild of the one, the first great-grandchild of the other. But before they had made ready to start upon the journey a letter was received from the child's mother saying that he had been taken dangerously ill. The two grand-mothers were greatly troubled and more anxious than ever to see the baby. The older one was in her bedroom, not feeling well; her daughter was with her. A vehicle was heard to drive up to the front door. Glancing from the window the younger grandmother saw it was the express wagon and a box was being lifted out, evidently for them. Thinking—its mother having said they should see it dead or alive—it contained the corpse of her baby grandchild, she hurried down, had it carried into the parlor and set upon a table. She then threw a white sheet over it and awaited in trembling and grief the home-coming of her husband—my father.

"When he came in she told of the box and its supposed contents, and he, also full of grief, set to work to open it. The lid was at length torn off, and great was the surprise and relief of both to come upon the fresh green leaves and berries beneath them.

"But the door-bell rang again, and there stood Hannah with her babe in her arms alive and well.

"Joyful was the welcome given to both; they were taken into the parlor, Hannah shown the box, which was still standing, and told the story.

"After a while the baby was allowed to trot about at his own sweet will, while the older people were taken up with each other (a cradle had been brought down to the parlor to lay the baby corpse in before the box was opened, and there it stood covered with a spread or something white), so when the little chap was left unnoticed, he got at the box of berries, carried some to the cradle and threw them in on the dainty white spread."

The little girls had been listening to their father's story with as much interest as if they had never heard it before, though doubtless it was quite familiar to them.

"Wasn't it funny?" asked one of them with a merry laugh, as he finished.

But just then a boy came running, calling out, "Pap, you're wanted now. Please come right away, mother says," and with a pleasant "Good-by, ladies," the father rose, took Sally in his arms and went, the rest of the children following.

## CHAPTER XVIII.

THE old soldier and his children had hardly left the vicinity of our young friends when Calhoun came to them with the glad news that Croly had so far recovered as to be able to speak naturally and recognize his friends, that his parents had been told of his danger and his rescue, and were now with him, weeping over his sufferings, rejoicing that he had been spared to them, and full of gratitude to Dr. Conly for his long-continued and untiring efforts for his resuscitation.

"I am proud of my brother and don't believe there is a better physician in the United States," concluded Calhoun, his eyes shining. "But, ladies and little folks, I just remember that Cousin Elsie charged me to tell you that dinner will be on the table in about ten or fifteen minutes."

"Oh, that's good news, Cousin Cal!" exclaimed Rosie, "for I'm pow'ful hungry, as the darkies say. There's nothing like sea-air to give one an appetite." And with that they all started for the house.

Arthur was longing to be with Marian, but at the urgent request of the elder Mr. Croly and his wife, consented to stay with their son, who had been carried to his uncle's cottage, through the rest of that day and the following night.

Then assuring them that Will had almost entirely recovered and there was no longer the slightest need of his services, he was beginning to bid them good morning when Mr. Croly, laying a detaining hand on his arm, poured out earnest thanks for the service he had done them in saving the life of their only and well-beloved son, and delicately asked what was his charge for his services, hinting that both he and his wife thought it should be a heavy one.

"Oh, no, sir," said Arthur, "I make no charge whatever for so trifling a service to one whom I had learned to love almost as a brother. I am more than repaid by his spared life—the blessing of God upon my efforts," and with a pleasant good-morning he hurried away.

He met the family at the breakfast table and was received with joyful greetings. An hour later he and Marian sought the beach together. It seemed a long time that they had been kept apart, and they greatly enjoyed being again alone together for a time.

When the mail was brought to the house Walter, as usual, came running down to them with their share—one letter for Marian and several for the doctor.

Glancing at his he noticed that one was without a postmark, and somewhat curious to know whence it came, he opened that envelope first. It proved to be from the elder Mr. Croly, and contained a note and another paper. Arthur opened and read the note first. In it the writer stated that he felt that he owed a debt of gratitude for the spared life of his only and well-beloved child which he could never by any possibility repay, and that the doctor who had been instrumental in saving that life would confer a favor by accepting the inclosed certificate of stock as a small token of the grateful affection of Will Croly's parents and of the dear boy himself, who would be delighted to have him do so, and feel that it was far from being an adequate return for the inestimable service rendered. The writer added that they would all feel sadly hurt should he refuse. All this Arthur read with a pleasant glow of feeling. " They are far more grateful than most people," he said to himself as he opened the accompanying paper.

" Can I believe my eyes?" he exclaimed mentally as he hastily glanced over it, then gave it a more careful examination.

The certificate was for stock to the amount

of one hundred thousand dollars yielding six per cent; there could be no mistake, and he felt that he had suddenly become a rich man.

But at that instant a low sob from Marian caught his ear, and instantly everything was forgotten but that she was in trouble.

" My darling, what is it?" he asked, putting an arm about her and drawing her closer to him.

" Oh, I am so frightened!" she said with quivering lips. " Read this letter from Sandy."

He did so at once. The boy wrote warning Marian that their father had in some way learned that Captain Raymond had shown himself a friend to her, so suspected that she had gone to him for protection, had found out the captain's address, and started east with the probable intention of hunting her up and carrying her back to Utah with him.

" Oh, what can I do? Can you protect me from him?" asked Marian, as Dr. Conly refolded the letter and drew her closer into his arms.

" He shall never take you from me," he returned in determined tones and holding her close to his heart. " I think the surest thing will be for us to marry at once, if you are willing. O my darling, you are not afraid to trust me?"

"No, no, i ideed!" she exclaimed, adding, "if you are willing to take me just as I am, only half educated and——"

"More, much more than willing," he replied. "But there is no time to be lost. Let us go up at once to the house and consult with the friends there."

"Yes; especially Cousin Elsie, and my best and kindest of friends, dear old Cousin Ronald."

They were glad to find all the family in, and quickly told them their story; Arthur concluding with, "I think the best thing we can do is to marry at once, so that I shall have a prior right to that of Mr. McAlpine, and can prevent him from carrying her away from us."

"I agree with you, sir," said Mr. Lilburn, "and should think it well for you to carry her away to some place unknown to the unnatural man, till he wearies of his search and goes back to Mormon-land."

"Then, if the plan is approved by my wife and others, I will go at once for the *Dolphin*, and we will sail or steam away to-night with the bride and groom," said the captain. "We can visit Mount Desert and whatever other points we please along the whole coast between this and our city, making occasional calls here if we like, and go home when we wish and are satisfied that the danger there is over."

"Oh, by all means let us go!" said Violet: "nothing could be more delightful."

"And Herbert and I will drive in at once for a minister to perform the ceremony," said Harold, taking up his hat. "Have you any choice, Marian?"

"I know none of them but the one to whose preaching the rest of you have been listening, and who kindly called to see me the other day," she replied with a blush.

"Then we will go for him," returned Harold.

"But stay a little, Harold," said his mother; "dinner is just ready, and you will have time enough afterward."

The summons to the table came at that moment and all answered it promptly.

At the conclusion of the meal the captain, Harold, and Herbert drove into the city—the first to see that all was right with the yacht and order it brought that afternoon to the landing nearest the house, the other two in search of a minister to perform the ceremony that was to unite Marian and the doctor for life.

"Now," said Rosie as soon as they were gone, "we must help the bride dress. Come, mamma and Violet, your help will be needed, for it is well known and freely acknowledged that you both have excellent taste."

"Ah," sighed Cousin Ronald, "I am sorry

18

there is no time for furnishing a handsomer trousseau. But fortunately it can be done afterward."

"No, no, dear Cousin Ronald, I have plenty of fine clothes," said Marian. "You have been so, so good to me."

At that Dr. Conly, remembering the munificent fee he had received that morning, smiled quietly to himself; but not a word did he say to any one about it. He felt that words could not express his appreciation of Mr. Croly's generosity to himself and others instrumental in the saving of his son's life; for he had learned from Harold that the men in the boat that picked up the nearly drowned young man had each been liberally rewarded, the one who drew him from the water especially so. Calling his Cousin Elsie aside, "Can we have any invited guests, do you think?" he asked with a humorous smile.

"Guests?" she repeated, with a look of surprise. "I hardly know where to find them in time for so hastily gotten up a ceremony."

"The Crolys are near at hand," he suggested.

"Oh, yes! invite them if you wish to," she returned with an amused laugh. "But we cannot get up anything like a proper wedding-feast on so short a notice."

"Oh, I dare say they will make due allowance

for haste, and expect little entertainment besides a good look at the bride," he said laughingly.

"Then I will send them a note of invitation. Also one to the younger Mr. and Mrs. Croly and to our poor friend Will."

"Cousin," he said with a joyous look, "I have something for your ear alone; other relatives and friends shall know of it by and by." Then he read her Mr. Croly's note and showed its inclosure.

"Oh, Art, I am so glad, so very glad!" she said, her eyes full of happy tears. "Yes, my dear fellow, give them all the warmest of invitations, though I hardly think Will or his father or mother will come; but they shall have the warmest of welcomes if they do."

"Is not that your place as mistress of the house, Cousin Elsie?" he asked.

"Oh, yes!" she replied. "I will write a note at once and send it by one of the servants."

"And, if you please, I will send a note of thanks along with it. I will write it at once."

"I will send it with pleasure," she said. "Oh, Cousin Arthur, I am so glad for you! It is not an extravagant gift for a man of Mr. Croly's means—and I think you have fairly earned it—but it must make you quite rich."

"It does indeed," he said in joyous tones, "and will put it in my power to make the dear girl who is trusting her happiness to me very comfortable. It will also enable me to help those of my brothers and sisters who may need aid."

"You have always been a generous fellow," she said, giving him a look full of appreciation and affection, "but I think if they do all they can to help themselves they will need very little assistance from you. But," she added with a smile, "we have each a great deal to do in a little time and must not hinder each other."

The delegation sent to the city was very successful. The young men returned early in the afternoon, bringing the minister of Marian's choice, and shortly after the captain came in from his yacht, which lay at anchor at no great distance from the shore.

Neither Will Croly nor his mother ventured out, but his father came, bringing his sister-in-law with him.

Marian looked very sweet and lovely in white tarletan and orange-blossoms brought by Harold from the city; and Arthur, still rather youthful in appearance, seemed a not unsuitable bridegroom for her. Mary Keith, Rosie, and Lulu, Calhoun, Harold, and Herbert acted the parts of bridesmaids and groomsmen.

The ceremony was short and followed by some

simple refreshments—several kinds of cake, ice-cream, and lemonade.

Trunks had been packed and sent aboard the yacht, and before sundown the passengers followed; the bride and groom, Calhoun and Mary, and the captain with his entire family. It was not at all a sad good-by to either those who went or those who stayed behind, for it was expected that the *Dolphin* would touch frequently at that port, so that her passengers could pay a visit to the friends on shore, often on their return taking some of them for a short distance out to sea.

The evening air from the sea was very cool, and for Marian's sake—she being as yet not far from on the invalid list—the older people confined themselves most of the time to the saloon. But Lulu, wrapping a shawl about her shoulders, went out upon the deck, where she seated herself and gazed silently out upon the sea.

They were steaming northward scarcely out of sight of the shore. It was a beautiful night, the moon shining brightly in the dark blue of the heavens, flecked here and there with soft, fleecy, white clouds, and the sea beneath looking like molten silver where her rays touched it.

Lulu enjoyed the sight and the delicious breeze that was blowing softly shoreward, yet

her thoughts were on other matters and she
was unusually silent and still. She had no one
to talk to, but was very apt when alone at such
time and place to sing softly to herself.

She had not moved for some minutes when
she felt a hand laid gently on each shoulder,
while her father's voice asked in affectionate
tones, "What is my little girl thinking of?"
He bent down over her as he spoke and she
looked up into his face.

"Oh, I'm so glad you have come, papa!" she
said.

"Are you, daughter?" he returned, coming
around, seating himself by her side, and putting
an arm about her waist. "I don't know when I
have seen you so perfectly quiet and still. A
penny for your thoughts."

"They're not worth a penny, papa," she said
laughingly, laying her head on his shoulder and
looking up lovingly into his eyes. "I'm afraid
they were rather foolish, but you can have them
for nothing if you want them. You know I
belong to you—I'm so glad I do—so you have a
right to my thoughts; haven't you?"

"We will leave that question to be considered
at another time," he returned laughingly, hugging her up closer and giving her a kiss; "but
since you are willing, you may tell me what was
the occasion of so much grave thought in this

little careless head," stroking her hair and repeating his caress.

"Well, then, papa, it was mostly about Marian I was thinking, and that I should not like to be in her place. I like Cousin Arthur ever so much for a doctor, but to have to leave my dear father and go to live with him instead would be just dreadful. But then her father can't be one bit like mine, and I think that if I were his daughter I'd be glad enough to leave him for Dr. Conly."

"And I think no one could reasonably blame you if you were; especially if, as in Marian's case, it was to escape being forced into a marriage with one who was far from agreeable to you and had already several wives—which is a very wicked thing, forbidden by the law of both God and man. But, situated as you are, it would, I think, be a very silly thing for you to do as Marian has done, even were you of her age, and you are really some three or four years younger."

"And that's a very great difference," remarked Lulu soberly, "and I'm glad of it, because I do so like to be my father's own little girl. And you won't ever make me get married if I don't want to, will you, papa?"

"No, daughter, certainly not. I shall be only

too glad to keep you—have you always and altogether my own."

"It's so good of you, you dear papa," she said, nestling closer to him. "I feel almost sure I shall never love any other man half so well as I do you."

"That is pleasant news to me," he said, with a smile down into the large, dark eyes lifted to his.

## CHAPTER XIX.

The next morning after the sailing of the *Dolphin* brought to Mrs. Travilla the news that her son Edward and his family, accompanied by Ella Conly, were on their way north, intending first to visit the Lelands at Evelyn's cottage on the Hudson, then to come on to spend a few weeks with her at the sea-shore.

Everybody was glad, for the departure of so large a number of those who had made up their family for weeks past had left them all feeling somewhat lonely.

Hugh Lilburn felt very loth to leave just as his betrothed was coming, for the visit on the Hudson was not to be a long one; besides, he was unwilling to leave his father to encounter Mc-Alpine without being there himself to defend him in case the Mormon should become abusive.

That he decided in his own mind would be worse than allowing his business interests to suffer somewhat by a prolonged absence from his newly acquired property.

But it was growing late in the season; the cottage nearest to the house occupied by the Dinsmores, Mrs. Travilla, and the others of that party was rented by them for the expected ones from New York, and in a week from the departure of the *Dolphin* and her passengers they arrived and took possession.

But they were much like one family, taking their meals at the larger house, spending the greater part of the day there or on the beach, or taking walks and drives together.

They had letters now and then from the party in the yacht, who seemed to be enjoying themselves greatly, and in a week after this last arrival the vessel touched at Gloucester, and Mary Keith, Calhoun, Herbert, and Harold landed, spent a few hours in the city, then returned to their sea-side home, where they were welcomed with demonstrations of delight.

They reported that Arthur and his bride seemed to be having a delightful honeymoon and deemed it best to remain on the yacht somewhat longer, unless they should hear of the whereabouts of McAlpine and know that they would be safe from a visit from him, which, unless he became a changed man, would undoubtedly be far from pleasant.

"I told them," said Calhoun, "that I should rather enjoy giving him a piece of my mind."

"Yes, probably rather more than he would," laughed Harold.

"I dare say," returned Calhoun, "but I can't

say that I am particularly anxious or desirous
to give him pleasure.   However, I think he will
find us too large a party to attack with anything
worse than hard words; and those I am by no
means unwilling to stand for the sake of my
pretty young sister-in-law."

"Marian is a sweet girl," said Mary Keith,
"and as Dr. Conly's wife she has made certain
her escape from a dreadful fate."

It was after tea and they were all in the parlor; for it was a cool evening, cloudy and occasionally drizzling a little.

Mary had scarcely ceased speaking when a
loud peal from the door-bell startled every one.
Harold stepped out to the hall to answer it.
There stood a tall, broad-shouldered man, who
accosted him with, "How do you do, sir?   I
understand that this is the house occupied by
Mrs. Travilla, Captain Raymond, and others."

"Mrs. Travilla is here; Captain Raymond is
not," returned Harold.   "May I inquire what
is your errand to either of them?"

"Yes.   I understand that they are harboring
here a daughter of mine, considerably under
age, who ran away from me some months ago.
I have come to take possession of her; and let
me say I intend to do so, let who will object."

"She is not here," answered Harold.

At that the man pushed him suddenly and

rudely aside and walked boldly and defiantly into the parlor. Mr. Lilburn instantly rose and faced him. "William McAlpine, what brings you here?" he asked in stern tones.

"Is it you, Ronald Lilburn?" exclaimed the other in astonishment. "I thought you were in auld Scotland and probably under the sod long ere this. And is it you that's carried off my bairn?"

"I have never seen Mormon land and didna carry her off," was Mr. Lilburn's reply in a tone full of scorn and contempt; "but if I'd had the chance I wad hae rescued her at the risk o' my life from sic a fate as you—unnatural beast o' a mon that ye are—had prepared for her. You are worse than a heathen, William McAlpine, wi' your three or four wives; and you broke the heart o' Marian's mither, my ain sweet cousin, who demeaned hersel' to marry you—a mean fellow not fit to wipe the dust from her shoon."

At that the man turned white with passion and lifted his clinched fist as if about to strike the old gentleman down. But his son Hugh sprang in between them, and at the same instant Edward and Harold sprang forward and each seized an arm of the stalwart stranger, while Herbert and Calhoun showed themselves ready to assist in preventing him from harming their old friend.

But at that instant a woman's voice, seemingly coming from the next room, spoke in sadly beseeching tones:

"O Willie, Willie, wad ye harm my own dear auld cousin who has never shown aught but kindness to us and ours? Is it not enough that ye broke the heart o'y ain wife that loved ye better than all the warld beside? And wad ye kill my ain bairn—the bonny lassie that we baith loved so well when she was a wee toddling thing? Dinna meddle wi' her, Willie; dinna harm a hair o' her head or I'll haunt ye to the last day o' your life. Forsake your sins, Willie, put away your mony wives and be a true servant o' the Lord, or ye'll never win to heaven; your soul will be lost and I that loved ye so lang syne will see ye no more forever."

McAlpine's face turned ghastly white while he listened and his eyes seemed starting from his head; then as the voice ceased he suddenly wrenched himself free from the hold of Edward and Harold and rushed from the room and the house like one pursued by an avenging foe; they heard his steps echoing down the garden path, out into the road, and away till the sounds were lost in the distance.

Then Mr. Dinsmore spoke, breaking the astonished silence:

"He is badly scared, and I think will hardly

return to pursue his search for his missing daughter."

"I trust not, sir," responded Cousin Ronald. "Fortunately I was able to remember and reproduce the tones of his dead wife's voice. My God-given talent is sometimes useful, as well as a source of amusement to my young friends."

"And older ones also," Elsie added with a smile.

"Yes, indeed," said Rosie; "the man fairly frightened me, for he acted as if he were wicked enough to hurt or even kill every one of us. I don't wonder Marian ran away from him and was so frightened at the very thought of seeing him again."

"Nor I," said Zoe, looking at her husband with eyes full of tears. "O my dear Ned, I was so afraid he would do you some dreadful harm! And what if he should even yet; he may come back! Oh, let us shut doors and windows."

"I think there is hardly any danger of his returning," remarked Hugh Lilburn in a reassuring tone; "at least not to-night."

The other gentlemen agreed in that opinion, and the ladies were sufficiently reassured to be able to pass a comfortable night.

But though they were ignorant of the fact, McAlpine was in no condition to injure any of them or even to return to their dwelling.

In the darkness and the confusion of his mind, he had wandered from the path and fallen down a hill, landing on a bed of stones, striking his head on one of them so that he was insensible for some hours, breaking a rib and receiving internal injuries that proved fatal in a very short time. In the morning some one passing heard his groans, went for assistance, and he was carried into a house and a surgeon sent for, who after making an examination told him he had but a few hours to live, and if he had any affairs to settle he would do well to attend to them immediately.

McAlpine was thrown into great distress of mind by the announcement, and begged to have word sent to the house where he had been the night before, with an earnest request that Mr. Lilburn would come to him, for at least a few moments, as he had something he wished to say.

Shocked at the news of the man's condition, Mr. Lilburn at once hastened to his bedside.

"They tell me I'm a dying mon, Ronald Lilburn, and I maun ease my mind afore I die, wi' a word for my daughter Marian. Tell her for me that I own I've been a hard father to her, and was—O God, forgive me—a cruel, unfaithful husband to her mither after I turned Mormon. It's a lustful, wicked pretence o' a religion, is Mormonism, and I dinna want Sandy brought up to believe in it."

He paused from exhaustion, and Mr. Lilburn told of his plans for Sandy and the offers he had made the lad to educate and start him in life.

"God bless you for it," returned the dying man. "I find now my death is near that I care more for those two o' my bairns than I thought. And now I maun think o' my soul! O Ronald Lilburn, what must I do to be saved? Is there ony hope for such a sinner as I?"

"Yes, William. 'The blood o' Jesus Christ his Son cleanseth us from all sin,' and while there is life there is hope. Flee to Jesus, the sinner's friend, remembering his own words, 'Him that cometh unto me I will in no wise cast out.'"

"Lord, I come, I come; be merciful to me a sinner; save me for thine own name's sake," came in earnest, pleading tones from the dying lips; a few long-drawn breaths followed and the soul had fled.

The *Dolphin* was known to be far out at sea; word of her father's arrival and his speedy and unexpected death could not be sent to Marian, so the body was carried to an undertaker's and the next day quietly buried from there, Mr. Lilburn, his son, and the other gentlemen of the family attending the funeral services.

When at length the news reached Marian,

something of her early love for her father seemed to return to her.    She shed some tears over it, yet in a short time her grief was more than swallowed up in a sense of relief.

She was very, very happy with Arthur, who proved himself the kindest and best of husbands. It was not thought necessary that her father's death should be made known in their home neighborhood, and on her return she dressed as a bride.    Her husband had told her of his improved circumstances and was disposed to lavish upon her everything that heart could wish. But she was not extravagant in her tastes or desires, and he was satisfied to let her follow her own inclination in regard to that and the continuing of her studies with Captain Raymond, at least for a time.

That pleased the captain, and he was more than willing to receive her as a pupil when they should all return home and he resume his labors as instructor.

The entire family had now been let into the secret of Arthur's wonderfully large fee for his medical service to William Croly, and heartily rejoiced with him.

Dr. Dick Percival joined them for a week at the sea-side, after which all returned to their homes.

Calhoun had tried to induce his Mary to follow with him the example set them by his brother and Marian, and Hugh Lilburn let his Ella know that he would be far from objecting to making it a double wedding; but neither lady would consent. Each wished to go home first and make suitable preparations for the important event, Ella adding that Isadore and the other sisters and brothers would have reason to be hurt if she did not invite them all to be present at her wedding.

Mr. and Mrs. Dinsmore and Mrs. Travilla thought she took a proper view of the matter, as did Mary also, in regard to the time and place of her own nuptials.

So Calhoun took her to her own home and left her there, with the understanding that he was to return for her some weeks or months hence—the day having not yet been fixed upon.

But before leaving their sea-side home all spent a day there together. Naturally one of the principal topics of conversation was the approaching journey to their southern homes.

"I wish I could take you all with me in the yacht," said Captain Raymond, addressing the company in general, "but unfortunately there is not accommodation for so many. Mother, we must have you and Grandpa and Grandma Dinsmore, as it is a more restful way to travel than by the cars. The doctor and his bride are already engaged to us, and we must, I think, take Evelyn, Rosie, and Walter; we should hardly know what to do without them any longer," he added with his pleasant smile. "We have eight family and passenger state-rooms, and beds can be made up at nights in the saloon," he continued, "and in that way we can make room for several more."

He paused for a reply, but no one spoke, each seemingly waiting for the others.

At length Violet said: "I think you and your babies should be with us, Zoe; then of course Edward would need to be there to take care of you all; for he would not be willing to trust that business to any one else. And Harold and Herbert ought to be with their mother, having, poor little lads! been so much away from her for the last few years," she added in a sportive tone.

Every one approved, and so it was settled. The journey was a safe and prosperous one with all; they arrived at their homes, Ion, Woodburn, and Roselands, without accident or loss, and presently had settled down for the duties and pleasures of the fall and coming winter.

THE END.